Time seemed suspended as their gazes met, his reflecting the same flare of heat that burned in her veins.

"I want to walk you to your room," he said.

Lauren drew a steadying breath and shook her head. "You're way too—"

"Irresistible?"

"I was thinking more along the lines of persistent." The elevator door opened on her floor and she moved forward onto the plush carpet.

Alex stepped off the elevator and the door closed behind him. He picked up her hand and drew a lazy pattern on her palm with his index finger. "I'd give up if you told me to get lost and meant it."

His touch made it difficult for Lauren to breathe. "I'm not sure."

"Maybe this will help you decide."

He tugged her toward him, and covered her mouth with his own.

Dear Reader,

What are your favorite memories of summer? Even though I spend my days reading manuscripts, I love nothing better than basking in the sun's warm glow as I sit immersed in a great book. If you share this pleasure with me, rest assured that I can make packing your beach bag *really* easy this month!

Certainly, you'll want to make room in your bag for Patricia Thayer's *A Taste of Paradise* (SR #1770), part of the author's new LOVE AT THE GOODTIME CAFÉ miniseries. Thayer proves that romance is the order of the day when a sexy sheriff determined to buy back his family's ranch crosses paths with a beautiful blond socialite who is on the run from an arranged marriage. Watch the sparks fly in *Rich, Rugged...Royal* by Cynthia Rutledge (SR #1771) in which an ordinary woman discovers that the man whom she had a one-night affair with is not only her roommate but also a royal! International bestselling author Lilian Darcy offers an emotional tale about an estranged couple who are reunited when the hero is named bachelor of the year, in *The Millionaire's Cinderella Wife* (SR #1772). Finally, I'm delighted to introduce you to debut author Karen Potter whose *Daddy in Waiting* (SR #1773) shows how a mix-up at a fertility clinic leads to happily ever after.

And be sure to leave some room in your bag next month when Judy Duarte kicks off a summer-themed continuity set at a county fair!

Happy reading,

Ann Leslie Tuttle
Associate Senior Editor

Please address questions and book requests to:
Silhouette Reader Service
U.S.: 3010 Walden Ave., P.O. Box 1325, Buffalo, NY 14269
Canadian: P.O. Box 609, Fort Erie, Ont. L2A 5X3

Rich, Rugged ...Royal

CYNTHIA RUTLEDGE

SILHOUETTE *Romance*®

Published by Silhouette Books

America's Publisher of Contemporary Romance

To Lee Cades, my favorite aunt

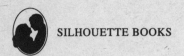

SILHOUETTE BOOKS

ISBN 0-373-19771-3

RICH, RUGGED…ROYAL

Copyright © 2005 by Cynthia Rutledge

This edition published by arrangement with Harlequin Books S.A.

® and TM are trademarks of Harlequin Books S.A., used under license.
Trademarks indicated with ® are registered in the United States Patent
and Trademark Office, the Canadian Trade Marks Office and in other
countries.

Visit Silhouette Books at www.eHarlequin.com

Printed in U.S.A.

CYNTHIA RUTLEDGE

is a lifelong Nebraska resident. She graduated from the University of Nebraska with a liberal arts degree, then returned several years later to earn a degree in nursing. A registered nurse, Cynthia now works full-time for a large insurance company and writes in the evenings and on weekends. She loves writing romance because a happy ending is guaranteed!

Cynthia loves to hear from readers and encourages you to visit her Web site at: http://www.cynthiarutledge.com.

Lauren's To-Do List:

* Develop pictures from friend's wedding.

* Remember fondly how I spent the wedding reception dancing with a handsome stranger... who is now my roommate.

* Eat a hot fudge sundae to forget that your roommate is a hunk and that you are "just friends."

* Go to Neiman Marcus and find a sexy dress on the off chance hot roommate will ask me out for a spontaneous dinner.

* Buy stamps so that I can pay overdue bills.

* Eat another hot fudge sundae to forget overdue bills.

* Go to Neiman Marcus to buy shoes I can't afford to match dress on off chance my princely roommate will find me irresistible.

* Eat third hot fudge sundae to numb the fact that I am in love with my roommate!

Chapter One

"Were there any men at the wedding?" Clarice Carlyle took a tiny bite of dessert and tilted her head expectantly, an avaricious gleam in her eye.

Lauren resisted the urge to sigh. Why couldn't her mother realize that not everything in life revolved around men? The fact that she was almost thirty and still unmarried drove her mother crazy. But she wasn't going to settle for just anyone. Or marry for money, as her mother hoped.

Lauren wanted the fairy tale. She wanted a man to sweep her off her feet, to love her with a passion that defied logic. Quite simply, she wanted to live happily ever after.

"They didn't invite any men," Lauren said flatly when the silence lengthened and she realized her mother actually expected an answer to the ridiculous question.

Clarice looked askance for a second before she chuckled. "Of course there were men there. Chicago is full of men. What I was asking was if you'd met anyone interesting?"

"I danced with several different men." Lauren skirted the question, her answer honest as far as it went. Most of the evening *had* been spent either talking or dancing with old college friends.

"Didn't anyone in particular catch your eye?"

Lauren sipped the Guatemalan coffee blend and hoped the heat stealing its way up her neck didn't give her away. One particular man had done a lot more than catch her eye.

"What's his name?"

"Who?" Lauren took a bite of cheesecake, desperately wishing she'd left right after dinner.

"The man who is making you blush," Clarice said. "I assume he was good-looking?"

Good-looking?

An image of Alex's face flashed before Lauren. Good-looking would be an understatement. She'd always liked men with dark hair. And Alex's hazel eyes held flecks of gold and green in their depths. At just over six feet, he was tall enough without being too tall, with a lean, muscular body and broad shoulders. In his arms, a woman could feel soft and feminine and utterly desirable.

"He was handsome," Lauren said into the expectant silence. "But it doesn't matter. I'll never see him again."

Having a one-night stand was one thing. Lauren wasn't going to compound the error by pretending the interlude had been about anything more than sex.

Clarice made a tsk-tsking sound. "You always were such a pessimist."

"Realist," Lauren said.

"If your father and I taught you anything," Clarice said. "It should be that where there's a will, there's a way."

"He's in Chicago, Mother," Lauren said, wondering why she continued to take part in this awkward discussion. It wasn't as if the cheesecake was *that* good. "Even if I wanted to get in touch with him, I wouldn't have a clue how to do it."

Clarice leaned forward. "Surely some of his friends were at the wedding?"

"He was an old college roommate of Tom Alvarez." Lauren shrugged. "That's all I know."

It wasn't, of course, all she knew, just all she was willing to share. Her mother didn't need to know what Alex looked like naked or that he spoke French when he made love.

"Tom Alvarez." Clarice's brows drew together. "Why does that name sound familiar?"

Lauren sighed. Tom had lived in St. Louis for several years and Clarice had met him on more than one occasion. Apparently he hadn't been high enough on the social ladder to warrant remembering. "He's Christy Warner's publicist."

"Of course." Clarice smiled. She certainly remembered the popular motivational speaker and her husband. "You should call Christy. Or David. I'm sure they'd help you track him down."

"No way." On this, Lauren would brook no argument.

Four years ago David Warner had been the man Lauren had planned to marry. Then, on a weekend trip to Las Vegas, he'd married his old high-school girlfriend on a whim. Lauren had long since forgiven them both and they were now all friends, but the last thing she wanted was for Christy or David to think she was so desperate she'd chase after a man who hadn't cared enough to ask for her number.

No, she may have behaved foolishly this weekend, but she was no fool.

"What does this mystery man do for a living?" her mother asked.

Lauren took a bite of dessert, getting an odd sense of satisfaction from knowing she was about to burst her mother's bubble. "He's unemployed."

The excitement in her mother's eyes dimmed but a flicker of hope remained. "Independently wealthy?"

Alex had driven her to the airport in a late-eighties Buick. Lauren smiled wryly and shook her head.

"Deadbeats." Clarice shook her head in disgust. "They're everywhere. Well, I wouldn't lose any sleep over the guy. He was probably married, anyway."

"He's *not* married," Lauren said. She'd always believed marriage vows were sacred. That's why she'd checked out his ring finger when he'd asked her to dance. And when he'd accompanied her up to her room, she'd asked him point blank.

"Don't get in a huff." Her mother took a sip of her coffee. "Most good-looking men are married. It's a fact of life."

"He's not married." Lauren's self-control snapped. "I would never have been with him if he was."

"Been with him?" Clarice stopped stirring the cream into her coffee and lifted a perfectly arched brow. "You were intimate with this man?"

Lauren's cheeks burned under her mother's suddenly curious gaze but she did her best to act nonchalant. "Goodness, no. We danced a couple of times. Had a few drinks and talked."

Though Lauren had never been much of an actress, she must have been successful because disappointment skittered across her mother's face. "That's all?"

"What?" Lauren's voice rose. "You think I should have slept with the guy?"

"I wouldn't have faulted you if you had." Her mother lifted a shoulder in a slight shrug. "I wanted you to have a nice weekend. If that included a little fling with a handsome man, I wouldn't have a problem with it."

If that included a little fling, I wouldn't have a problem with it.

Lauren pressed her lips together and pulled into the driveway to her town house. She'd beaten herself up for behaving recklessly while her mother obviously saw nothing wrong with it.

Of course, that should have come as no surprise. Her mother had always been into living for the moment and doing what felt good. Though Lauren had always abhorred that philosophy, last weekend she'd embraced it with a passion that still made her blush.

And it had been surprisingly easy.

All it had taken was one look across a crowded ballroom....

Lauren's lips lifted in a slight smile and she raised her glass in a mock salute. She'd noticed the man earlier on the dance floor. The first time, he'd been chatting with a perky blonde with an irritating laugh.

The second with Joni Alvarez, who'd smiled a greeting at Lauren as she'd whirled past in his arms.

Lauren had been intrigued but didn't think he'd even noticed her. Until her gaze had scanned the ballroom later in the evening and she'd found him staring. A shiver traveled up her spine as he handed his empty glass to a waiter and started across the room.

In a matter of seconds he was at her side.

"Care to dance?" His husky voice kicked her heart into high gear.

Lauren lifted one shoulder in a slight shrug and set her drink on a table. "Why not?"

The minute he took her hand and pulled her close she realized her mistake. Just being in his arms made Lauren's blood run hot and her body ache with longing. And judging from the desire flickering in his eyes, he wasn't immune to their close proximity, either.

They danced together for three songs before Lauren made her excuses and said goodbye. The way she was feeling, staying any longer would be dangerous.

Lauren exited the Grand Ballroom, crossed the hotel lobby and headed for the elevators. She decided it had to be the wedding that had stirred up all these disturbing feelings of…well…lust.

Sara Michaels, one of her friends from St. Louis, had sung at the wedding and the songs of love had stirred up feelings Lauren normally kept deeply buried. It hadn't helped that at the reception everybody seemed to have someone. Everybody except her.

She sighed and reached for the elevator button.

"Let me get that," a familiar deep voice murmured.

Lauren glanced up and her eyes widened in surprise. The last she'd seen Alex, he'd been surrounded by several young women who seemed to be hanging on his every word. "Are you calling it a night, too?"

"I'm not staying at the hotel," he said.

The elevator door opened and he waved his hand for her to precede him, then followed. "I just thought it'd be a good idea if I walked you to your room."

Lauren frowned. She may have laughed a lot when they were dancing, but she'd only had a couple of glasses of wine and was totally sober. "I can make it to my room on my own just fine. I don't need an escort."

"I didn't say you did." He shot her a wink. "This is solely for my pleasure."

Though she liked being with him, liked talking to him, Lauren wasn't sure having him walk her to her room was a good idea.

"You know, if it makes any difference, I don't bite."

His grin was so infectious that Lauren couldn't help but play along. The door slid shut and Lauren punched her floor. "How can I be certain of that?"

"Because—" he took a step closer "—if I did bite, I would have taken a nibble or two out of you on the dance floor."

Without a word of warning, he moved closer and his fingers delved through the warm, silky mass at the nape of her neck and his thumbs grazed the soft skin beneath her jaw.

Her breath caught in her throat. Time seemed suspended as their gazes met, his reflecting the same flare of heat that burned in her veins.

"I want to walk you to your room," he said again.

Lauren drew a steadying breath and shook her head. She wasn't sure she trusted him. Or was it herself? "You're way too—"

"Irresistible?"

"I was thinking more along the lines of persistent." The elevator door opened on her floor and she moved forward onto the plush carpet.

Alex stepped off the elevator and the door closed behind him. "Everyone has a few faults."

"Being impulsive has never been one of mine," she said.

He picked up her hand and drew a lazy pattern on her palm with his index finger. "I'd give up if you told me to get lost."

His touch made it difficult for Lauren to breathe, much less think clearly. "I'm not sure—"

"Maybe this will help you decide."

He tugged her toward him, reached with his right hand to pull her chin up and covered her mouth with his own.

His lips were warm and sensual, the scent of him musky and all male. The late evening stubble on his cheeks lightly chafed her skin, eliciting a stirring of desire in her blood. Her heart beat hard and fast in her chest. He lifted his head and met her gaze, his eyes dark and intense.

Lauren exhaled a slow breath as they stared at each other. She wanted this man in a way that defied logic. All she knew for certain was that the feeling was honest and true.

Now, all she had to do was decide whether to trust her instincts….

The ring of her cell phone jarred Lauren back to the present. For a second she felt cheated, as if the unexpected phone call had interrupted something important. Until she remembered, that night in her hotel room she and Alex hadn't been interrupted…by a phone call or anything else. It had just been the two of them, undisturbed, all night long.

Chapter Two

Lauren glanced around the trendy St. Louis coffee shop and wondered if any of the other patron's lives were in such a mess.

"My life is spiraling out of control," Lauren said with a sigh to her friend, Sara Michaels.

Sara sipped her Italian soda and focused her gaze on Lauren, her blue eyes curious but not alarmed. She lifted a perfectly shaped brow. "Don't tell me Nordstrom decided to not put their coats on sale this week?"

"I wish that's all it was," Lauren said with a sigh. "Unfortunately it's way more serious."

Surprise flitted across Sara's face. "What's going on, Lauren?"

Lauren hesitated. Now that the moment was at hand, the words wouldn't come. The Christian singer was her best friend and Lauren's moral compass. Though she had no doubt her friend would be shocked and disappointed, Lauren knew Sara would be just the one to help her sort through her tangled emotions.

Goodness knows Lauren couldn't count on her parents for that kind of help. If only she could follow her mother's suggestion and simply forget the guy. But the problem was Lauren couldn't forget him. The memory of their time together was as vivid now as it had been when he'd dropped her off at the airport and they'd said their goodbyes.

"Lauren?" Sara flashed an encouraging smile.

Lauren traced a crack on the tabletop with one finger and forced a casual tone. "Have you ever done something you knew at the time was wrong, but you went ahead and did it anyway?"

A strange expression crossed Sara's face. Instead of answering immediately, she took a sip of her soda and her eyes took on a faraway look. After a long moment, she nodded.

"I don't need specifics." Lauren leaned forward and rested her elbows on the table. "But whatever it was, if you had it to do all over again, would you?"

"At the time I thought it was justified," Sara said. "But I was young. In retrospect it was definitely the wrong thing to do."

Lauren wasn't sure what Sara's sin had been, but knowing her friend's propensity for doing the right thing, whatever it was couldn't have been all that bad. Nothing on the order of a one-night stand. Still, it was good to know that Sara could understand how a person could stray from the straight and narrow.

"I did something recently." Lauren waved a hand in the air, being deliberately vague. "Even at the time I knew it was wrong. But I went ahead and did it anyway."

"And now you're sorry." Sara's voice softened with understanding. She leaned forward and gave Lauren's hand a squeeze. "At one time or another we all do things like that, things we're not proud of, things we regret."

Lauren stifled a groan. Sara had missed the point. It wasn't regret that haunted her thoughts, but the absence of regret.

"The thing is, I *don't* feel bad," Lauren said. "I know I should, but I don't. And, worst of all, given the chance I'm sure I'd do it again."

A frown furrowed Sara's brow. "I don't understand."

"It's my mother," Lauren said. "I'm starting to think I'm just like her."

Sara's gaze shifted to the bulging sacks of clothes next to Lauren's chair. When Lauren got wound up, nothing soothed her like walking down the aisles of a department store perusing the merchandise, trying on clothes, mixing and matching. Sara, like the rest of Lauren's friends, understood that shopping was her way of dealing with stress.

Lauren nudged at the sacks with the toe of one shoe. The only thing she regretted about the clothes was that she'd have to take most of them back. The high rent she paid on her luxury town house took most of her paycheck and her credit card couldn't handle much more.

"Lauren." Sara's voice was low and filled with compassion. "You haven't been yourself since you got back from Chicago. Did something happen there?"

"Chicago was fun," Lauren said, avoiding the question. "It was great seeing everyone again."

Still, the event had been bittersweet. Lauren had been happy for her last unmarried girlfriend. And she'd been equally happy for her other college friends with babies on their hips. But she couldn't help but wonder when it would be her turn. When would she have a man of her own? And a child to hold in her arms?

"Tell me why you think you're just like your mother," Sara said when Lauren didn't elaborate.

Lauren stared down into her cup then lifted her gaze to Sara. "She sees what she wants and she goes for it, regardless if it's a wise course of action or not. Lately I've been doing the same thing."

"That's not true." Sara's response said more about her loyalty than her ability to be realistic when it came to her friends.

"It *is* true. I've leased a town house I can't afford." Lauren decided that sounded better than saying she'd had a one-night stand with a man she'd never see again. "And I'm constantly buying clothes I don't need just because I want them."

Her gaze dropped back to the sacks at her feet.

"If this is about money," Sara began, "I have some extra and I'd be happy to—"

"Absolutely not," Lauren said firmly. Taking money from friends was her father's specialty. She'd sleep on a park bench before she'd accept a dime from Sara. "But I do have to get a roommate. So, if you know anyone who might be interested, send them my way."

Sara leaned back in her chair, her expression thoughtful. "I might know someone. The only problem is, he's a guy."

Lauren resisted the urge to smile. Who, but Sara, would worry about such a thing? "That doesn't bother me. I lived in a coed dorm in college."

"I'm not sure how long he'll stay in St. Louis but he *is* looking." Sara raised a finger to her lips. "And I think the two of you would get along."

Lauren raised a brow, her curiosity piqued. "Do I know this guy?"

"He's not from here," Sara said. "I've just hired him to handle the arrangements for my upcoming European tour."

"Is he cute?" The question popped out of Lauren's mouth before she could stop it.

"I think he's attractive," Sara said. "But then I've always been partial to guys with dark hair and hazel eyes."

Lauren smiled. Sara's husband, Sal, a hunky ex-cop, fit that description to a *T*. So did Alex.

An image of Alex flashed before Lauren. Though it had been almost a week since their time together, she still found herself waking up at night and thinking about him. Even now, just the thought of him rekindled her desire.

Lauren shoved the memories aside. If she did get a male roommate, part of the ground rules would be that there would be nothing personal between them. Otherwise it would never work.

"How well do you know this guy?" Lauren asked. "I mean, I don't want to worry about living under the same roof with Jack the Ripper."

Sara chuckled. "This guy is definitely no Jack the Ripper. Both Tom Alvarez and his previous employer couldn't say enough nice things about him. That was the reason I decided to interview him in the first place. I have to say I was impressed. And he passed muster with Sal."

Sara's eyes softened, the way they always did when she mentioned her husband. She'd been married for almost three years to the former undercover cop and Sal guarded his wife and baby daughter's privacy with the zeal he'd once reserved for his police work. If he approved of this new guy, the man must be okay.

"Is he even looking for a roommate?" Lauren asked. "Maybe he wants a place of his own?"

Sara lifted the cup to her lips and paused. "I think he'd prefer a roommate. Money seems to be an issue."

"Not paying him enough?" Lauren teased.

"According to my manager, I'm paying him too much," Sara said with a laugh. "But he had great qualifications."

"So why would money be an issue?"

"I don't know." Sara gave a shrug. "We didn't get into his personal life. But a few things he said led me to believe he's watching his pennies. It struck me as odd at the time because the clothes he wore were very stylish and definitely not off the rack."

"Sounds like my kind of guy," Lauren mused. Though the man would only be living under her roof and they wouldn't necessarily have to be friends, it was reassuring to know they shared a love of nice clothes. "When do you think I could meet him?"

Sara's eyes widened and she lifted a hand in a gesture of greeting. "How about right now?"

"Now?"

"He just walked through the front door."

Lauren swiveled in her chair. Her heart stopped at the sight of the tall, broad-shouldered man making his way to their table.

"Alex," she breathed the word, feeling suddenly light-headed.

Chapter Three

Lauren saw the flash of recognition in Alex's eyes and the watchful look that replaced the smile he'd bestowed on Sara.

"What a surprise." Sara's smile widened as he drew close and she gestured to the empty chair at their table. "Won't you join us?"

"I'd love to." Casting Lauren a questioning glance, Alex pulled out a chair and took a seat.

He was absolutely gorgeous. The cream-colored button-up shirt accentuated his tan and made his eyes look even darker. His brown dress pants were definitely hand-tailored and, if she wasn't mistaken, the belt encircling his waist cost more than all the clothes in her sack combined.

As she'd relived their night together in her memory, Lauren had convinced herself that he couldn't have been as handsome as she'd remembered. She'd decided that the late hour, the wine and the stress had clouded her recollection. But she'd been wrong. His features were chiseled, his nose long and aristocratic. His chin was strong and his lips perfectly sculpted.

His sun-streaked brown hair gleamed in the coffee shop's subdued lighting. He wore it conservatively short but it was thick and wavy and almost begged for her fingers to run through the strands again.

"Alex, this is my good friend, Lauren Carlyle," Sara said. "Lauren, Alexander Gabrielle. Alex is co-ordinating my European tour."

Lauren met Alex's gaze. From the watchful look in his eyes, she knew that he was willing to take his lead from her. It didn't take even a second for her to decide how to handle the situation.

"You look familiar." Lauren extended her hand. "Didn't we dance together a couple of times at Melanie's wedding?"

"I think you're right." He grasped her hand and brought it to his lips. "Enchanté."

She shivered as he placed a kiss on the back of her hand, feeling her cheeks redden.

"I should have warned you, Lauren." Sara laughed, a silvery tinkle that reminded Lauren of tiny bells. "Alex is very European."

Lauren widened her gaze, truly surprised. "You're not American?"

He smiled and gestured for the waiter, ordering an espresso before turning his attention back to her. "Actually I have dual citizenship. My father is American while my mother is a citizen of Carpegnia."

"Carpegnia?" Though Lauren knew the location of practically every Nordstrom store in the United States, geography had never been her strong point. "Is that in the Mediterranean?"

Alex nodded. "Off the southern coast of France."

"But you don't have an accent," Lauren said.

He smiled. "Sometimes I do."

Ma chérie.

When they'd made love, he'd whispered the words over and over. Lauren took a deep breath. "So you speak English and French?"

"Along with several other languages," he said as if it were no big deal.

"When I interviewed Alex, I knew he was just what I was looking for," Sara said. "Not only is he fluent in all those languages, he's very familiar with Europe."

"I know it intimately," Alex said. Was it only her imagination or had his deep, sensual voice lingered on the last word?

Lauren's heart skipped a beat but she cast him a warning glance. Sara was smart and if he wasn't careful, she'd catch on that her new employee and her old friend knew each other better than they were letting on.

"Your espresso, sir." The waiter placed the cup before Alex, smiled and turned on his heel.

"Lauren is in the market for a roommate," Sara said as soon as the waiter left. "She asked if I knew anyone who might be interested and I mentioned you were looking."

"Roommate?" That cute little dimple she remembered so well flashed in Alex's cheek, and Lauren decided she'd be safer with Jack the Ripper under her roof.

"It's very small," Lauren said.

"Your town house is spacious," Sara protested. "And quite lovely."

"We'd be tripping all over each other," Lauren added.

"I don't mind being close." Alex took another sip of his espresso but mischief gleamed in his eye. "Not at all."

Sara's brows pulled together in puzzlement and Lauren kicked Alex under the table.

"The extra bedroom and bathroom are in the *basement*," Lauren said.

Actually, the downstairs area was light and airy with huge daylight windows. But there was no need for Alex to know that.

"Sounds cozy." Alex didn't appear the least bit dissuaded. "I like cozy."

He winced as the pointed toe of her shoe connected with his shin once again.

"I'm sorry, but I just noticed the time." Sara pushed back her chair and rose to her feet. "I have to pick up the baby."

Alex rose to his feet. "Are we still on for seven?"

Sara hesitated a fraction of a second. "Absolutely."

Lauren hid a smile. It was obvious that her friend had completely forgotten the plans. Since her baby had been born, Sara's already hectic schedule had kicked into overdrive and she'd confided in Lauren that half the time she didn't know whether she was coming or going.

Sara shifted her gaze. "Lauren, I'd love to have you join us. Sal's mother sent over some lasagna this morning and I'll probably just throw together a salad. You haven't been over in forever. Please say you'll come."

Lauren squirmed in her chair. She couldn't imagine being in the same room with Alex all evening. Even now the electricity between them was almost palpable. "I'm not sure tonight will work."

"C'mon, Lauren." Sara put a hand on her hip and her lips came together in a pout. "You told me earlier you didn't have anything going on this evening."

Lauren glanced at Alex and found him grinning.

"We'll eat at seven," Sara said as if the matter were already decided. "Sal will probably want to go over some of the tour's security requirements with Alex after dinner. That'll give us the opportunity to continue our talk."

Lauren offered a noncommittal smile. Alex's appearance had effectively ensured that her night of passion in Chicago would remain her secret.

Unless Alex decided to talk….

Lauren waited until her friend was out the door before she turned back to Alex. "What is going on here?"

Alex stared unblinkingly, the anger in her voice taking him by surprise. He'd gotten the impression she'd been glad to see him. Now he wasn't sure. "What do you mean?"

"You told me you were unemployed."

"I also told you I was interviewing for jobs," he said.

"You could have told me you knew Sara."

"I had no idea you two were friends," he said. "I was as shocked as you when I walked in and saw the two of you together."

Actually, shocked didn't begin to describe how he'd felt when he'd glanced across the crowded coffee shop and saw Lauren sitting at the table with his new boss. For one crazy second, he'd wondered if his job was over before it had begun. Sara was a devout Christian and even though Alex believed he had in no way taken advantage of Lauren, he knew Sara might not see it that way.

"I take it you didn't tell her about us?" Though Sara's comments had led him to believe that was the case, Alex had to know for sure.

For a second she hesitated. His heart dropped until she rolled her eyes.

"Get real. What was I going to say? Hey, Sara, I know how you feel about sex before marriage. Want to hear about the one-night stand I had last weekend?"

He chuckled but quickly sobered at the warning look in her eyes.

"No one knows about that night," Lauren said. "I want it to stay that way."

"I understand," Alex said.

"I don't think you do." Lauren leaned forward and lowered her voice, resting her elbows on the table. "My friends have high moral standards. The school where I teach is very conservative. This can't get out."

"You're right. Teachers don't have sex." Alex tried not to smile, but he couldn't quite pull it off.

Her lips pressed together. "Be serious."

She looked so cute with her emerald eyes blazing and a rush of pink staining her cheeks that he was tempted to tease her some more. But the lines of worry edging her eyes stopped him.

He met her gaze. "No one will hear about it from me."

"Thank you." Her sigh was clearly audible.

"But if your friends are as conservative as you say," Alex said. "What are they going to think about us living together?"

"It doesn't matter," Lauren said. "I've decided it's not a good idea for us to be under the same roof."

The same thought had crossed his mind. Alex needed this job and he couldn't afford to get on Sara's bad side. Living in the same house with her friend would be just asking for trouble.

A sensible man would drop the subject and go back to reading the want ads. But Alex had never been particularly sensible and he'd never liked the idea of living with a stranger.

Lauren wouldn't be a stranger….

She'd remained in his thoughts since that night in the hotel. Alex had cursed himself for failing to get a phone number or address. He'd thought it would be so easy. When he arrived in St. Louis he'd look up her name in the phone book and give her a call. The only problem was there had been no listing for a Lauren Carlyle. Just when he'd reconciled himself to the fact that he'd never see her again, their paths had crossed. It seemed like fate.

"I don't see the problem," Alex said in his most conciliatory tone. "It will be strictly a business arrangement. You need the money. I need a place to live."

"I know this may be hard for you to believe—especially after how I behaved the other night but I usually don't have trouble keeping men at arm's length," she said. "It's different with you."

He could sense her cryptic comment was significant, so he pondered the words for a moment before speaking. "So you're saying you think you could be under the same roof with another man and it'd be okay? But not with me?"

Her blush deepened. "We've been intimate."

"I realize that." Alex met her gaze. "But we're also adults with free will."

Lauren leaned back in the chair. "It happened once. I don't want it to happen again."

Actually, he wanted to remind her, it had happened twice, not once. And the problem seemed to be that she *did* want it to happen again.

He smiled reassuringly. "I've already promised that when I move in, I'll keep my distance."

Though Alex truly meant the words, he wondered how long he'd be able to keep that promise. Even now, keeping his distance wasn't that easy. She was so pretty with her dark hair brushing her shoulders and her large almond-shaped green eyes. Her ivory skin was smooth and clear and if she had any flaw at all, it was her charming tendency to blush at the slightest provocation.

Spending the next six months with her would be a pleasure. Even though he'd have to pay for the privilege, Alex thought with a wry smile.

"Why don't you give me the grand tour?" Alex asked. "If it's acceptable, we'll talk money."

Up until this year he'd never had to give a thought to what things cost. Now he did nothing *but* think about it. It seemed so gauche; such bad form to talk dollars and cents. But he had no choice.

"That's not going to work," Lauren said.

Alex frowned. "What's not going to work? Giving the tour today? Or waiting to discuss money?"

"Both," Lauren said. "I'm telling you for the last time. There's no way you're moving in."

Chapter Four

After leaving Alex at the coffee shop, Lauren returned home to find a stack of bills in her mailbox. For a moment she was tempted to subscribe to her mother's out-of-sight, out-of-mind philosophy and toss 'em into the trash. Instead she put them on the desk, where they joined all the other statements waiting to be paid.

A sick feeling washed over her. Broadview Academy only paid their teachers monthly and the check she'd just gotten was already gone.

If she let Alex move in, she'd have all sorts of money. Maybe even enough left after paying bills for that cashmere sweater at Nordstrom...

She shoved the crazy thought aside and reminded herself that Alex wasn't her only option. St. Louis was a big city. There had to be any number of respectable men and women looking for a place to live. All she had to do was find one.

Two hours later, Lauren was less optimistic but not dissuaded. She'd called every person she could think of asking if they knew of a potential roommate for her. Her gaze drifted back to the stack of bills. The problem was she couldn't really afford to wait around hoping one of the "possibilities" that had been mentioned would pan out.

The shrill ring of the phone kicked her heart into overdrive and renewed her hope. She snatched the phone from the cradle and prayed it was one of her friends calling back to say they'd found someone who was interested in the room.

The credit-card companies would be happy and she could almost feel soft cashmere against her skin. "Hello."

"Lauren." Surprise echoed in her mother's voice. "I didn't think I'd catch you at home."

Lauren stifled a groan. She'd have preferred a telemarketer.

"I was prepared to leave a message."

"I could hang up and let it go to voice mail," Lauren offered.

Her mother laughed, apparently not realizing

Lauren was serious. "Your father and I want you to come to the house for dinner tonight."

Lauren paused, instantly suspicious. Her parents always entertained their friends on the weekend. Not to mention she'd just been there for dinner.

"It's Saturday," Lauren said finally. "I assumed you'd be having people over."

"We are," her mother said pleasantly. "But there's no rule that says our daughter can't be one of the guests."

"Thanks for the invitation," Lauren said. "But I already have plans."

"A date?" her mother asked, surprise evident in her tone.

"Actually I'm going over to Sara's for dinner."

"Tell her you'll come another time," her mother said as if that settled the matter. "Did I mention that your father met the nicest man at the Club the other day? He thinks the two of you would be perfect for each other."

Suddenly all the pieces fell into place.

"Let me guess," Lauren said. "This nice man just happens to be coming to dinner tonight?"

"As a matter of fact, he is," her mother said with obvious satisfaction. "He's a great catch—thirty-three, moderately attractive and runs his own business. A business, I might add, that has been very successful. Best of all, he's unattached."

"Unattached?" Lauren couldn't keep the suspicion from her voice.

"He soon will be," her mother said. "He's in the process of filing for divorce."

"He's married?" Despite Lauren's intention to keep emotion out of the conversation, her voice rose.

"You weren't listening," her mother said in a lighthearted tone. "He's already met with an attorney. The timing couldn't be more perfect. Did I mention he's an entrepreneur?"

"Yes, you did." Lauren congratulated herself on keeping her tone even, though she was seething inside. "But as I said, I'm not able to make it tonight. And, even if I were available, I'm not interested in married men."

"He's not married," her mother protested. "He's—"

"I know," Lauren interjected. "He's filing for divorce. I'm not interested in dating those kind of men either."

Her mother sighed. "You're never going to find anyone decent with that attitude."

Silence filled the phone line.

"Lauren, honey." This time her mother's tone was conciliatory. "You can have dinner with Sara anytime. I know you'd like Chad if you'd just give him a chance. But timing is crucial. You need to snatch him up while he's available."

Lauren thought about reminding her mother the guy really wasn't available, but knew her comment would fall on deaf ears.

"I'm not changing my plans." Lauren wondered for the hundredth time how she'd ended up with such parents. They were basically nice people but they had a strange way of looking at the world.

Opportunistic was the word she'd settled on back in high school when her father had almost gone to prison for investment fraud. She'd decided it sounded better than amoral or criminal.

"And I'm not interested in your latest prospect." Lauren added in case her mother still hadn't gotten the message.

"He'll be here at seven," her mother said as if Lauren hadn't spoken. "Wear something pretty. And low cut. Might as well show off your assets."

"I'm not comin—"

"See you at seven."

The dial tone sounded and Lauren resisted the urge to strangle the phone. Why couldn't she have had a normal mother? Marion Cunningham of *Happy Days* would never have tried to fix Joanie up with a married man. Olivia Walton would have never tried—

Lauren forced the comparisons from her mind and reminded herself she had more important things to worry about than her mother and her ridiculous matchmaking.

She had bills to pay.
And a roommate to find.

Living out of a hotel room had never been a problem for Alex. In fact, he'd spent six weeks at the Ritz in Boston just last year while he visited his youngest brother.

But his seven days at the Inn-and-Out Motel had been seven days too many. The place reeked of garlic from the restaurant next door and the paper-thin walls made sleep impossible. If it wasn't the baby down the hall crying for hours on end, it was the couple in the next room making loud passionate love.

Not only had the moans kept him awake, they'd brought back memories of the night he and Lauren had shared.

Though he'd be lying if he said he didn't want her in his bed, what Alex really wanted was to get to know her better. He wanted to hear her laugh. He wanted to see her cheeks turn a becoming shade of pink. He wanted to be her roommate.

She might have made her home sound less than appealing but Alex knew she'd just been exaggerating in an attempt to dissuade him. The place had to be a step up from the motel room and whatever she charged him in rent would be a whole lot cheaper than what he was paying for this dump.

Being without a job for four weeks had been

enough to deplete most of the money Alex had managed to save the past five months. Of course, he still had ten thousand dollars set aside in a Chicago bank, but he'd starve before he'd touch a dime of those funds.

Alex's gaze drifted to the clock he'd placed on the room's rickety desk. His eyes widened. There was no time to waste. He needed to be at Sara's house in Brentwood in less than an hour and he still had to pack.

Tonight was his chance.

He had to convince Lauren she'd made a mistake.

And more importantly, he had to convince her to take him home.

On her way to Sara's house Lauren decided she was sick of winter. Though her friend never complained about the weather, Lauren knew the snow and cold had to be wearing on her, too. That's why stopping at a florist's shop made perfect sense. Fresh flowers would be just the thing to add a breath of spring to the evening's festivities.

Thankfully, the Stem Gallery had in-store credit so Lauren was able to give her charge card a much needed rest and walk away with a bigger bouquet in the bargain.

The sweet scent of flowers filled the tiny interior of Lauren's car and brought a smile to her face. A smile that turned thoughtful when she pulled up in front of Sara's house and saw Alex's car parked in the driveway.

Though every self-preserving bone in Lauren's body told her to keep her distance from the man, she couldn't stop the anticipation that coursed up her spine at the thought of seeing him again.

And the fact that she'd just checked her makeup before leaving home didn't stop Lauren from flipping down the vanity mirror. But she told herself the fact that Alex was waiting inside didn't have a thing to do with her desire to do a last minute touch-up. She always tried to look her best, no matter what the occasion or who was in attendance.

She applied more color to her lips, grabbed the flowers and headed up the walk.

Sara's husband opened the door before the bell rang twice, a warm smile of welcome on his lips. Sal quickly ushered her inside, taking the flowers and her coat.

Alex must have just arrived because he still stood in the foyer chatting with Sara as if she were an old friend instead of his new employer.

Sara's hand rested lightly on his arm and she gazed up at him in rapt attention. Despite being dressed in basic black, the singer resembled an angel, with her silvery blond hair and big blue eyes. A fact that hadn't escaped Alex's notice. Even from a distance, Lauren could see the admiration in his eyes.

A swift stab of jealousy took her by surprise.

"Look what Lauren brought me." Sal shot his wife a teasing grin and held out the bouquet.

Sara shifted her gaze and her smile widened. She moved quickly across the foyer and gave Lauren a hug.

"It doesn't surprise me." Sara's blue eyes sparkled with good humor. "I always knew she had a thing for you."

Lauren watched the playful interplay, wishing her mother were standing here to see the happiness the two exuded. Maybe then she'd understand that this was the kind of relationship Lauren wanted, one with true love driving the commitment, not money.

"They're beautiful." Sara took the flowers from her husband and nimbly darted out of reach when he attempted to pull her close. "I'm going to put these in a vase. Sal, would you hang up their coats and then help me get the salads on the table?"

Lauren resisted the urge to look at Alex. The moment her gaze had settled on him, a curious longing filled her. She couldn't deny she found his quiet confidence and classic good looks appealing. But the last thing she wanted was for him to know it.

"Where's Anna?" Lauren looked around, finding the house strangely silent.

"Miriam is feeding her upstairs," Sara said. "She's cutting teeth and has been a little fussy."

Miriam Wilkins was a retired woman from Sara's church who helped out with household duties and childcare on a part-time basis. The fact that she was busy with the baby explained why Sara was on her own with dinner preparations.

"I hope Miriam doesn't keep her up there all evening," Lauren said. "I don't care if she's fussy."

"That's easy for you to say," Sal said with a long-suffering sigh. "But fussy doesn't begin to describe how she's been the last few days."

"I'd be glad to take her off your hands," Lauren bantered back, knowing there was no chance of that happening. Anna Tucci was the apple of her father's eye. "Just say the word."

"The word is no." Sal took Alex's coat and draped it over the one Lauren had given him. "If you want a baby, Ms. Carlyle, you're going to have to get your own."

Lauren gave him a playful shove. "I think I should find myself a husband first, don't you?"

Sal just laughed and waved her and Alex off in the direction of the dining room before heading to help his wife in the kitchen.

Lauren walked down the hall next to Alex, feeling as unsure as a teenager on her first date. The awkwardness took her by surprise. After all, they'd parted on good terms and they hadn't had any trouble communicating last weekend.

The memory of how she'd fallen into his arms so easily still made her blush. That's why she kept her gaze focused straight ahead and did her best to act cool. Unfortunately his close proximity and the familiar scent of his cologne wafted about her, stirring her senses, taking her back to that morning in the hotel room....

The knock at the door roused Lauren from a deep slumber. She opened her eyes.

"Stay in bed." Alex came out of the bathroom, a towel wrapped around his waist. His hair was damp from the shower and tiny beads of water still clung to his chest. "I'll get it."

Lauren realized with sudden horror that the dreams she'd had last night were this morning's reality.

"Wait—" Lauren called out, an image of her friends standing in the hall flashing before her.

"It's just room service," Alex said, opening the door. "I called before I got in the shower."

A young man carrying a silver tray stepped into the room and cast a surreptitious glance at the bed.

Lauren slid lower in the bed and resisted the urge to pull the covers over her head, her face burning with embarrassment.

Alex handed the employee several folded bills, took the tray and shut the door after him.

"I hope you like bacon and eggs," Alex said.

"I don't feel like eating," Lauren said.

She couldn't believe she'd been so reckless. So impulsive. She barely knew the guy but yet they'd made love. Not just once, but a second time during the night.

Thankfully he'd had a condom.

The first time.

A chill traveled up her spine.

Alex's eyes darkened and desire filled their depths. Just like it had last night. "If you'd rather—"

"The second time." Lauren paused and took a steadying breath. "Did you use a condom?"

Lauren was almost certain of the answer but she clung to a tiny shred of hope. She'd tried to keep her tone casual, but the tremble in her voice gave her away.

A myriad of emotions skittered across Alex's face. "I only had one condom in my wallet. We used it that first time. I didn't even think—"

"You didn't think?" Her voice rose and anger mixed with raw fear.

Alex raked his fingers through his hair and blew out a harsh breath. "It just happened. I rolled over and there you were. Suddenly we were kissing and…"

He let his voice trail off but Lauren didn't need him to finish; she'd already filled in the blanks. And as much as she wanted to put all the blame on him, she knew it had been as much her fault as his.

"I don't know a delicate way to put this." Lauren picked at the edge of the sheet. "So I'm just going to ask. Is there any possibility you could have any diseases? Or anything else I should know about?"

"I'm clean." The serious look on his face told her she wasn't the only one who realized the gravity of the situation and her respect for him inched up a notch. "How about you?"

"I'm clean, too," she said.

"You're on the Pill."

It was more a statement than a question and completely understandable given her age and single status. But the fact was until last night she'd had no need for birth control. She hadn't slept with anyone since a brief affair several years ago and her cycles were like clockwork.

The importance of that observation struck Lauren like a lightning bolt. Her breath came out in a whoosh and she felt almost giddy with relief. She couldn't have picked a better time of the month to have unprotected sex.

"I'm not on the Pill," she said, talking quickly when she saw the look of shock on his face. "But it's okay. Really."

He started to speak but she continued without missing a beat.

"Trust me." She put as much conviction in her voice as she could muster. "You have *absolutely* nothing to worry about."

Lauren hoped he would just accept her assurance but the look on his face told her it wasn't going to be that easy.

"I don't understand." His brows pulled together and she could see uncertainty in his gaze. "If you're not on the Pill, how can you be so certain there's nothing to worry about?"

Knowing he deserved more detail didn't make the words come any easier. Lauren tucked her hands beneath the covers and took a deep breath.

"I'm very regular and this was a good time—I mean there's never a good time not to be protected—but this was the best time if you had to pick a time. There's virtually no chance..."

She stopped suddenly, her cheeks burning like fire under his steady gaze. The words may have come out as a jumbled mishmash and the explanation might have been less than scientific, but she'd said all she was going to say. He was a smart guy. He could figure it out.

Dead silence greeted her words.

Lauren focused her attention on the gilded mirror hanging over the dresser.

"Are you sure?" he asked at last.

"Positive." The word might be a little too strong, but Lauren knew he wouldn't accept anything less than absolute certainty. Besides, she *was* positive. Practically positive.

She could hear him expel the breath he must have been holding. "I can't tell you what a relief that is."

"We were lucky," Lauren said, echoing the emotion. If this had happened five days later... She shuddered at the thought.

"Very lucky," he echoed.

"I don't know what got into me." Lauren shook her head, still unable to believe she'd taken such a chance.

"I know what got into me," he said, flashing a smile that took her breath away. "You."

Maybe it was the relief of knowing she didn't have to worry about pregnancy. Or the fact that one of the most handsome men she'd ever seen was intimating he found her irresistible. Whatever the reason, the comment struck her as hilarious and Lauren burst out laughing.

He frowned. "What's so funny?"

"You make it sound like you couldn't resist me." Lauren shook her head, a smile lingering on her lips, the thought too ridiculous for words.

"I don't know why you find that so hard to believe. You're a beautiful woman." His gaze lingered on her face, heating her skin. "And incredibly sexy."

Languid warmth filled her limbs at the look in his eye and she was filled with an overwhelming sense of gratitude. His words were a balm on her wounded spirit. She'd spent years dating a man who'd only thought of her as a friend and after that relationship had ended, she'd engaged in a couple of brief and totally unsatisfactory affairs.

She'd begun to wonder if the problem in the relationships had been *her;* her lack of sex appeal, her limited experience….

"I'm glad you decided to come tonight," Alex said.

The words pulled Lauren back to the present. She realized he'd pulled out her chair. She smiled and took a seat at the dining-room table.

"You look incredible."

Had she ever known a man who could put such a sexy spin on three simple words? Even though they weren't true.

In fact, she'd deliberately dressed down this evening. Though she had a new outfit hanging in her closet with the tags still on it, the last thing she'd wanted was for Alex to get the idea she'd dressed to impress. That's why she'd settled instead on a simple Donna Karan black skirt and jersey turtleneck. Last season's Fendi boots completed the ensemble. She looked chic, but not incredible.

"You look like you belong in New York." Alex took a seat next to her and his appreciative smile shoved her heart into overdrive. "Or Paris."

"You don't have to live in New York or Paris to be stylish," Sara said, unexpectedly breezing through the doorway and placing the salads before them. "I think you'll find we're actually quite cosmopolitan here in St. Louis. Lauren especially is always on the cutting edge of the latest trends."

Lauren tipped her head modestly. So many people thought of the Midwest as a cultural and fashion wasteland, when nothing could be further from the truth.

"You don't do so badly in that department yourself." Sal set the remaining salads on the table before pulling out his wife's chair.

"What can I say?" Sara laughed. "Like Lauren, I love to shop."

Lauren sighed. The difference was that Sara had the money to cover her purchases. Lauren didn't. Having her checking account in the red made even *talking* about her favorite pastime painful.

Focusing her gaze on Alex, Lauren deliberately changed the subject. "Sara said you've been all over the world. Did your previous job require a lot of traveling?"

"I've traveled a fair amount," he said finally, not really answering her question.

Lauren shot him an encouraging smile. After all, the other night they hadn't spent much time conversing and it was time she knew more about the stranger whom she'd slept with.

Chapter Five

Lauren discovered it wasn't easy to get someone to elaborate when you wanted to be subtle. In fact it was downright impossible. After all, how do you badger a man for details without drawing undue attention to yourself? And how do you make someone talk?

Ma chérie.

She took a ragged breath, remembering the way he'd murmured the words in that deep, husky voice of his as he'd scattered kisses across her belly.

"Lauren." Sara's voice broke through her reverie. "Are you okay? You looked positively flushed."

Though her heart had to be beating at least two hundred beats a minute and was probably going to burst apart any second, Lauren met her friend's concerned look with a bright smile. "I'm fine."

"Sara's right." The look in Sal's hazel eyes mirrored his wife's concern. "Your face is bright red."

"You do—" Alex started to agree.

Lauren shot him a quelling glance and he stopped short. Though Alex might not realize it, this was his fault. She wouldn't have gotten so hot and bothered if he wasn't in the room.

"I'm just a little warm." Lauren smiled and quickly improvised. "My house is so cold that when the thermostat is set at a reasonable level, I overheat."

Two tiny lines of worry appeared between Sara's brows.

"I could turn it down a little, if you'd like," Sara offered. "Sal tells me all the time I keep the place too warm. But it's been unusually cold this winter and I worry about Anna."

Lauren groaned. The last thing she wanted was to have a six-month-old get chilled. Especially when her flushed face had nothing to do with the temperature and everything to do with the man who sat to her right, a knowing smile on his lips.

"Don't you dare touch that thermostat," Lauren said hurriedly when Sara pushed back her chair. "I'm loving the heat. In my house I feel like I have to dress for outdoors while I'm inside."

It might have been a slight overstatement. After all, sweaters and socks were what most people wore during the winter months. But Lauren had always preferred shorts and a T-shirt when she was in the privacy of her house. Unfortunately her heating bill two months ago had put an abrupt end to that practice.

"How cold do you keep it?" Sal asked, stabbing a piece of lettuce with his fork.

Lauren sighed. "Sixty."

"Sixty?" Shock echoed in Sara's voice. "That's practically freezing. How can you possibly be warm when it's that temperature?"

Alex took a sip of water. "I bet Lauren knows a lot of creative ways to keep warm."

How Lauren kept the smile on her face, she wasn't sure. She only wished Alex was sitting across from her so she could give him a good swift kick in the shins.

"Actually I *have* learned a few tricks," she said, casting him a sweet-as-sugar smile. "I dress in layers, always wear socks on my feet and drink hot tea in the evening instead of anything cold."

Alex chuckled. "I'd just turn up the heat."

A lot of the teachers Lauren worked with said the same thing and if she had a few more dollars coming in, that would be her attitude, too. But when push came to shove, she wanted her morning caramel macchiato and scone more than she wanted to ante up to the gas company.

"Thankfully it's March." Sara picked up her fork and took a bite of her salad. "Spring is just around the corner."

"And before we know it, summer will be here," Lauren said.

"Let's not rush that," Sara said with a laugh. "My tour starts in July and we're still finalizing dates. But now that Alex is here, I'm hoping that everything will come together quickly."

"When do you start work?" Lauren asked, slanting Alex a sideways glance.

"I started Wednesday," Alex responded with a grin. "Sara put me to work immediately."

Sara wrinkled her nose. "I'm a slave driver."

"I can vouch for that." Sal laughed out loud and his wife's lips puckered in a pretty pout. "But I love her anyway."

The former cop leaned across the table, took his wife's hand and brought it to his lips.

It was an intimate moment, one that only underscored the devotion that existed between the two. A moment that reminded Lauren of the reason she didn't engage in meaningless affairs. True love was what mattered, not momentary thrills.

Despite herself, Lauren found her gaze drifting to her right where she encountered Alex blatantly staring. She immediately shifted her attention back to her salad, but the fluttering in her throat made it hard to swallow.

Somehow Lauren managed to choke down her food and make it through dinner. After they finished eating, they moved to the living room and Miriam brought the baby down.

"She is so adorable." Lauren cuddled Anna close and stroked the top of the baby's blond peach fuzz with the tip of her finger.

"We think she's pretty special," Sal agreed, his loving gaze resting on his daughter's face.

"Honey seems to have adjusted." Lauren's gaze dropped to the dog at her feet. The collie thumped her tail on the hardwood floor but didn't raise her head. Honey had been Sal's pre-wedding gift to Sara and the dog had been their baby until Anna arrived on the scene.

"She loves Anna," Sara said, favoring the dog with a smile.

Lauren's gaze lingered on the baby's sweet face. Inadvertently she found herself raising her voice to that high-pitched tone reserved for dogs and babies. "Who wouldn't love Anna Banana?"

Sara and Sal looked at each other and smiled.

"You really seem to like babies," Alex said. "I'm surprised you don't have one of your own."

It was an odd comment and if they'd been alone,

Lauren wouldn't even have responded. But with Sal and Sara sitting right there, Lauren felt compelled to be polite.

Lauren raised her left hand and wriggled her ring finger. "I'm not married," she said. "And even if I'd wanted to go the single route, I can barely support myself, let alone a baby."

"Hook up with a rich guy," Alex said, his expression inscrutable. "Women do it all the time."

Lauren had to laugh. "Now you sound like my mother."

· Alex lifted a brow and though he tried to hide it, Lauren could tell her comment had surprised him.

"Your mother?" Alex asked.

"You should meet Clarice," Sara said with a laugh. "When Sal and I first started dating, he was an undercover cop. The first chance she had, Lauren's mother pulled me aside and told me in no uncertain terms that I could do far better for myself."

Sara rolled her eyes, telling them all exactly what she thought of Clarice's comment.

Alex shifted his gaze to Lauren. "I take it she has equally high aspirations for you."

"If she had her way, I'd have latched myself onto the first wealthy man who crossed my path. But I have to say that today she reached a new low." Though a trace of a smile lingered on her lips, disappointment coursed through Lauren's veins. After all, this wasn't a quirky aunt she was talking about, this was her *mother.* "She tried to fix me up with someone who is still married."

Sara looked taken aback and blinked several times. "Married?"

"That's right. But he's a great catch and according to her, he'll be filing those divorce papers any day now." Lauren shook her head in disgust.

"Are you going out with him?" Alex asked in an offhand tone that Lauren guessed was anything but offhand.

"What do you think?" Lauren didn't even try to hide her irritation. Surely he could see she wasn't the type of woman to date a married man.

"I think it's time for us to go back upstairs," Miriam said brusquely, breaking the awkward silence and taking Anna from Lauren's arms. "This little lady needs her bath."

"Do you need any help?" Lauren asked.

Miriam smiled, her faded blue eyes filled with gentle understanding. "I think I can handle it."

The older woman had barely left the room when the doorbell rang.

"I wonder who that could be? I'm not expecting anyone." Sara looked at Sal. "Are you?"

Sal shook his head. He rose from the sofa, two hundred pounds of tightly leashed power. "I'll see who it is."

He'd barely left the room when Sara stood. "If you'll excuse me, I'll get the coffee and dessert."

"I'll go with you." Lauren started to rise but Sara waved her back down.

"Stay and entertain Alex," Sara said. "I'll be right back."

Lauren met Alex's gaze, letting him know by the look in her eye that she expected an apology.

But she was still waiting when the sound of a man's voice filtered into the room. Lauren groaned. Just when she thought the night couldn't get any more complicated…

Even before she saw his face, Lauren recognized the voice. She'd known Aaron "Rusty" Addison since she'd been in high school and he'd had a crush on her since he was sixteen. Oh, he'd dated a number of women through the years, but no one had been able to dislodge Lauren's place in his heart.

Rusty had suggested more than once that he and Lauren would make a perfect couple. She always just smiled and changed the subject. She liked Rusty, she really did, but only as a friend, nothing more. She couldn't imagine kissing him, much less ever being intimate with him. Rusty was the older brother she'd never had, her champion and protector.

His face brightened the way it always did the moment he saw her. He crossed the room in three long strides.

"Sal said he'll be back in a minute." Rusty's gaze lingered on her face in almost worshipful adoration. "He told me he had company. He didn't say it was *you*."

Lauren's heart couldn't help but warm. Rusty's smile radiated total and unconditional love. He'd always been her staunchest supporter.

When her longtime boyfriend, and Rusty's closest friend, had unceremoniously dumped her for another woman several years ago, Rusty had been aghast. He hadn't hesitated to tell David that he was a fool. At the time, Lauren thought her world had ended, but she now realized it had been for the best. David had never loved her as more than a friend and she deserved more. Rusty did, too.

She focused her attention back on the lanky redhead, noticing for the first time that he had on his work shirt; a long-sleeved gray polo with *Rusty* stitched in burgundy letters above the pocket. Rusty worked as a production crew chief for Warner Enterprises, a manufacturing firm owned by Lauren's old boyfriend.

Lauren lifted an eyebrow. "Working weekends?"

Rusty smiled and shrugged. "One of the guys got sick during second shift. I didn't have anything going tonight so I went in for a few hours to help out."

Lauren grinned. "Why doesn't that surprise me?"

Alex cleared his throat and Lauren realized that

sometime during the past few minutes he'd risen to his feet.

Rusty's gaze slid to him and his eyes widened in surprise. He shifted his gaze to Lauren for a moment before focusing once again on Alex. Lauren could see her old friend making all the wrong assumptions, but he handled the situation with surprising self-confidence.

"I don't believe we've met." Rusty's trademark smile quickly replaced his shocked expression. "I'm Aaron Addison, an old friend of Lauren's, and Sara and Sal. Most everyone calls me Rusty."

Alex shook Rusty's outstretched hand.

"Alex Gabrielle," he said in that well-controlled deep voice that sent shivers down Lauren's spine. "I'm in charge of Sara's summer tour arrangements."

Relief danced across Rusty's freckled face. "So you and Lauren aren't—"

"Lauren and I met briefly at a wedding last weekend," Alex said in an offhand tone that even she found believable. "We've been getting acquainted this evening."

Lauren expelled the breath she'd been holding. Everything Alex said was true—as far as it went. She didn't know why she'd been worried. After all, Alex had assured her he wouldn't let on just how well he'd known her from before. But something in his eyes a moment earlier had made her wonder. For a second he'd almost looked…jealous.

"Why don't you have a seat, Rusty, and tell me what you've been up to." Lauren gestured to the space beside her on the sofa.

"Don't mind if I do," the redhead said with a grin, plopping down so close to Lauren that barely an inch separated them.

Alex's gaze narrowed but he resumed his seat in a nearby chair and didn't comment.

"Did you find a roommate yet?" Rusty asked. "I got your message on my recorder but I didn't have a chance to call around. Although I do know that Sparks from the plant is looking. His wife kicked him out last week."

John Sparksman worked on the production line at Warner Enterprises and Lauren had met him and his wife at several of the spring galas that Warner Enterprises held annually for their employees. Up until a few years ago, Lauren had attended those occasions as David Warner's date and he'd always made it a point to speak to everyone at least once during the course of the evening.

Sparks had been one of her least favorite employees. She'd never liked his smile—which appeared to be more of a leer—or the way he looked at her as if she were a T-bone and he hadn't eaten in a week.

"I could talk to him," Rusty offered. "See if he's interested. I don't know why he wouldn't be. Your place would certainly be a step up from where he's living now."

"That won't be necessary," Lauren said, knowing she'd rather be evicted than let John Sparksman within ten feet of her house. "I—"

"I don't mind," Rusty said. "You sounded really desperate on the recorder. I'd be glad—"

"What Lauren is trying to say," Alex interjected smoothly, an easy smile on his lips, "is that she's already agreed to rent the room to me."

"I—" For one of the first times in her life, Lauren found herself speechless. She refused to let Sparks past her front doorstep, yet she had the feeling that the man sitting across from her might be even more dangerous, though in a far different way.

"You didn't tell me you and Alex had come to an agreement." Sara stood in the doorway, a pleased smile on her face. "I mean, I knew you two were discussing the matter but I didn't know it had been settled."

"What's going on?" Sal asked, appearing curious. He placed a tray of desserts and coffee on the side table.

"While he's in St. Louis, Alex is going to rent the downstairs of Lauren's town house," Sara said.

"Good." Sal nodded approval.

"I can't believe you're okay with a stranger moving in with her." Rusty's voice rose and his eyes flashed.

Sal's gaze narrowed.

"That's my decision to make, Rusty," Lauren said hurriedly. "Sal doesn't—"

"I can answer for myself, Lauren." Sal's tone was pleasant but his eyes were hooded and the smile had left his lips.

The former undercover cop clearly hadn't appreciated Rusty's tone of voice. Still, he held back.

Some of his restraint probably had to do with the fact that Sal knew Sara wouldn't appreciate a scene. But mostly, Lauren realized, it was because Sal knew Rusty.

It was common knowledge in their circle of friends that Rusty was Lauren's champion. If you messed with her, you answered to him.

"Lauren's right. She is a woman capable of making her own decisions, and I respect that. Both Sara and I do." Sal's voice held a steely edge. "But that said, Sara wouldn't have suggested Alex if we'd had any concerns about his character."

"But how do you know?" Rusty's gaze remained fixed on Sal. "Sara just hired him—"

"Alex is an old friend of Tom Alvarez," Sara said. "They roomed together in college. Tom couldn't say enough good things about him."

"And, of course, I did my own background check," Sal added.

Surprise skittered across Alex's face and Lauren could tell this was the first he'd heard of it.

"You did?" Sara moved to her husband's side and lifted a troubled gaze. "You never said anything to me."

His arm slid around her waist and he pulled her close. "I did it for my own peace of mind," he said softly. "I knew the person you hired would be spending a lot of time in the house with you and Anna. I needed to be sure I could trust him with my two best girls."

The expression on Sara's face softened and Lauren could tell Sal had redeemed himself.

"I still don't think it's a good idea for him to live with you." Rusty shifted his gaze to Lauren and lifted his chin in a stubborn tilt.

Lauren wasn't sure that having Alex live with her was a good idea either, but she'd never liked being told what to do. She fixed her gaze on the redhead. "As Sal said, it's my decision and I've made it."

Rusty started to argue but something in Lauren's expression must have caused him to reconsider. He stopped and heaved a resigned sigh. "So when is he moving in?"

"Tonight," Alex said, unexpectedly reentering the conversation. "My bags are in the car."

Chapter Six

Alex tried hard not to reveal the triumph surging through him. When he'd left the motel this evening with his bags piled in the back of the Buick, he'd been without a game plan.

His only goal was to have a place to stay by evening's end. Though he hadn't been particularly pleased when Rusty had shown up, the man's arrival had turned out to be key to his success.

"Tonight?" Rusty's voice rose. "What kind of person moves at night?"

"Someone who refuses to spend another minute at the Inn-and-Out Motel," Alex said with a wry smile.

Rusty's eyes widened. "The one on Woodson Road?"

"That's the one," Alex said.

"What a dump," Rusty said. "Sparks thought about staying there because it's so cheap, but it was too trashy even for him."

"Rusty." Lauren's voice rang with censure.

Rusty's ears turned bright red but he lifted his chin and met her gaze. "Have you seen the place?"

"No, but—" Lauren began.

"It's bad," Rusty said. "Real bad."

Lauren shifted her gaze to Alex. "Why would you stay in a dump?"

Embarrassment coursed through Alex. Being poor, even temporarily, was a new experience. Even in college the condo he and Tom had shared had been quite luxurious. "I knew I wouldn't be there more than a week or two."

"How long will you be staying with Lauren?" Rusty asked.

As a member of Carpegnia's royal family, dealing with nosy reporters was a part of life for Alex. He'd learned at an early age how to answer questions without really giving any information away and to conclude an interview when the person asking the questions began to annoy him.

He'd quickly reached that point with Rusty.

He stood and held out a hand to Lauren. "It's getting late. We'd better go."

Lauren ignored him. Her gaze drifted to the side table. "Sara made dessert. And coffee."

"Don't worry about that." Sara rose from the chair with a graceful elegance that Lauren had always envied. "I didn't realize Alex still had to move in this evening."

"He can wait until tomorro—"

"I've already checked out." Alex knew it was rude to interrupt but he couldn't wait for her to finish. He'd long ago learned the value of pressing an advantage. And he had the feeling that if he didn't move in tonight, he might not move in at all.

"There's a Motel 24 just off the highway," Lauren said. "I'm sure they have a vacancy."

"Lauren, don't tease him." Sara shot Alex a reassuring smile. "Now, a good hostess would probably never say this, but Anna was up most of last night and I'm really tired. Once you leave, I'll be heading straight to bed."

Alex hid a smile while Lauren's expression tightened. She had no choice and she obviously knew it.

She stood and fixed her gaze on Sara. "You're really going to bed?"

Sara nodded.

"Me, too," Sal added, shooting his wife a wink.

"If you need any help moving, I'll be glad to come

over and lend a hand." Though his words appeared directed to Alex, Rusty kept his gaze firmly on Lauren.

Alex fought back a surge of irritation. He didn't like the way the man's gaze lingered on Lauren and he resented the way Rusty kept trying to get involved in something that wasn't his concern.

"Thanks," Alex said. "But I don't have much. Just a couple bags."

"If you're sure…?" Rusty's gaze remained fixed on Lauren and Alex knew what he was asking didn't have a thing to do with the weight of the luggage.

Alex resisted the almost overpowering urge to answer for Lauren, to tell Rusty that of course she was sure. But he sensed Lauren wouldn't appreciate such high-handedness and that such a tactic might backfire. So Alex clamped his jaws together and remained silent.

Lauren hesitated for only a fraction of a second, but it seemed like an eternity to Alex.

"Rusty." When Lauren finally spoke, her voice was soft with understanding. "I'll get Alex settled into his room and everything will be fine."

The tension in Rusty's shoulders didn't ease at Lauren's words and Alex almost felt sorry for the man. Rusty would be even more upset if he knew Lauren's relationship with her new roommate wasn't going to be strictly business.

After all, Lauren had slept with Alex before. And Alex had no doubt that given time and the right situation, she would again.

Lauren rolled over in bed and stretched. Though she'd spent the minimum amount of time showing Alex around the town house last night, it had still been after midnight before she'd fallen asleep. She lifted a lazy gaze to the alarm clock. Her eyes widened and she jerked upright, suddenly wide awake.

Church started in forty-five minutes. That left her with only thirty minutes to get ready and on the road.

After a quick shower, Lauren pulled on a pair of black dress pants and a vintage russet-colored sweater; simple but definitely stylish.

She'd just started down the short flight of stairs to the main floor when she stopped. The aroma of freshly brewed coffee wafted up the steps, filling the air.

For a second, Lauren thought she must be hallucinating…until she remembered her new roommate. Taking a steadying breath, Lauren descended the rest of the stairs.

She came to an abrupt stop at the doorway to the kitchen. The normally immaculate room looked like a tornado had ripped through it. The door to the cabinet where she kept the appliances had been flung wide open. The toaster and coffeemaker were on the counter, a tub of butter and a carton of half-and-half between them. An open jar of strawberry jelly with the head of a knife sticking out sat on the stovetop and bread crumbs were everywhere.

Lauren took a breath and counted to ten before speaking.

"I assume—" she paused and cast a pointed glance at the mess "—that you're planning on cleaning this up?"

"Good morning." Alex smiled and gestured to the coffeemaker. "Would you like a cup?"

Alex's easy smile and wide-awake gaze told her he was one of those disgusting souls who embraced the dawn. If she'd had doubts about this arrangement working before, the fact that he was a morning person was the nail in the coffin.

Lauren was tempted to fling her arms to the heavens and ask God why he'd chosen to punish her in this way. She got up early because she had to, not because she enjoyed it. And she most certainly never smiled before her second cup of caffeine.

Still, the coffee did smell good….

"Maybe just a quick cup." She grabbed a mug from the cupboard and splashed a healthy dose of cream in along with a few cubes of sugar.

"Why are you all dressed up?" he asked, taking a bite of toast.

Lauren poured the coffee into the mug and took

a sip, savoring the robust flavor on her tongue. He'd made it strong, just the way she liked. She took another sip, glanced at the clock and decided she had time to sit for a minute. "I'm going to church."

"Church?" Alex couldn't have looked more startled if she'd said she was heading down to sell herself on the street corner.

"It's Sunday," she pointed out, filching a slice of toast smothered in jam from the plate in front of Alex. "Sara is singing at the early service."

Lauren didn't make it every week and when she did go, it was to the noon service. But when Sara had mentioned yesterday that she'd be doing a medley of some new praise music she'd written, Lauren had impulsively told her she'd be there to cheer her on.

"Is she any good?" Alex took another bite of toast.

"Of course she is," Lauren said. "You know that."

"Actually I've never heard her." He wiped a trace of jam from his lips with the corner of a napkin, appearing not the least bit embarrassed by the admission.

"But you're coordinating her tour." Lauren couldn't keep the shock from her voice.

"I imagine I'll hear her one of these days," Alex said with a shrug.

"I don't know how you can be effective in your job if you've never heard her sing." To Lauren's dismay, her voice rose with each word.

Belatedly she realized she was getting upset over something that was no big deal. She paused, took a deep breath followed by a long sip of coffee.

Alex studied her for a moment then smiled. "You want me to go to church with you."

"Absolutely not." Lauren sat her cup on the table with such force that coffee sloshed over the sides. She wiped the spill with a nearby napkin, wondering where he could have got such a crazy idea. Showing up with Alex would get everybody talking. "I was just saying sometime, not necessarily now. Maybe ask her to sing for you this week."

"No time like the present." Alex pushed back his chair and stood. "I'm ready to go."

Despite the fact that she had no intention of taking him with her, Lauren's gaze flickered over him, sharp and assessing. Dark pants. Crewneck sweater. It wasn't a suit, but Sal didn't always wear one to church either.

"Really, there's no need for you to—"

He raised a brow. "Are you saying you don't want me to go with you?"

If she were going anywhere but church, Lauren would have told him that's exactly what she meant. But telling someone they weren't welcome in God's house made her uneasy.

Alex smiled, apparently taking her indecision as agreement. "I'll grab my coat."

Lauren sank into the chair and took another sip of coffee. Getting up early had been her first mistake. She hoped showing up at church services with Alex at her side wouldn't be her second.

Chapter Seven

The church pews were hard, the sanctuary over-heated and the sermon long. Alex rose for the closing hymn and glanced sideways at Lauren. She caught his gaze and shot him an unexpected wink.

Alex decided he was glad he'd come.

Instead of wanting to stay and talk after the service concluded as he'd expected, Lauren seemed determined to get to the parking lot quickly and beat the crowd. They were making good time until she unexpectedly halted on the front steps. Alex obligingly stopped.

A woman with jet-black hair and too much makeup had a hand firmly wrapped around Lauren's arm. Fashionably thin, she wore a dress meant for a woman Lauren's age, rather than someone in their fifties. Nonetheless, she did exude a certain sense of style and a commanding presence.

Though Alex shifted his attention to the dispersing congregation to give the two some privacy, he couldn't help overhearing their conversation.

"Mother." Although there was a smile on her lips, Lauren's voice was tight with strain. "I didn't expect to see you here this morning."

"Why didn't you come last night?" the woman asked. "Chad was extremely disappointed."

"I had plans," Lauren said in an equally cool tone. "Besides, I thought I made it clear I had no intention of getting involved with a married man."

"His wife isn't even in the picture," her mother countered. "She's—"

"Drop it, Mother," Lauren said. "Not interested."

Alex could scarcely believe his ears. It was bad enough that her mother had tried to hook Lauren up with someone who was married. He couldn't believe she had the nerve to press the issue. He took a step closer to Lauren, resisting the urge to place a protective arm around her stiff shoulders.

For the first time, Clarice Carlyle appeared to notice her daughter wasn't alone. She immediately shifted her sharp-eyed gaze from Lauren to Alex. Surprisingly, some of her irritation seemed to ease at the sight of him. Her lips widened in a pleasant smile and she extended a perfectly manicured hand. "I don't believe we've met. I'm Clarice Carlyle, Lauren's mother."

Alex took her hand. "Alex Gabrielle. I'm coordinating Sara Michaels's European tour." He briefly considered adding that he was Lauren's new roommate, but instinct warned him to keep silent.

"Sounds important," Clarice purred, gazing up at him through lowered lashes.

"Not really." Alex refused to give her an ounce of encouragement. He'd encountered many such women over the years and her demure manner didn't fool him. Her calculating gaze had flicked over his clothes and come up with an impressive enough figure that he'd piqued her interest.

"It's a temporary position. When it ends I'll be unemployed. Again." He forced a heavy sigh, hoping that would be the end of it. Unfortunately her skeptical look told him she wasn't someone easily dissuaded.

"I'm sure a man of your obvious talents won't have any difficulty finding another position." She smiled and cast another calculating look at his Dolce & Gabbana sweater.

"The market is tough." Alex lifted a shoulder in a shrug. "If it wasn't for my friend Tom introducing me to Sara, I'd probably still be unemployed. Thankfully I've got friends who don't mind if I crash with them when money gets tight."

A momentary look of surprise flashed across Clarice's face. When her smile turned polite and the gleam left her eye, Alex knew his comments had hit the mark.

"Yes, well," Clarice said, her gaze searching the rapidly dwindling crowd. "I'd love to stay and chat but I see the mayor's wife and I absolutely must say hello."

She hurried off without another word, her heels clacking noisily on the concrete.

Alex watched the woman deliberately change her path to walk directly in front of a handsome man with silver hair, talking on a cell phone. It could have been a coincidence except for the added sway of her hips and the bright smile she flashed.

Alex could only stare. "She's just as I pictured."

Lauren sighed.

"What's your father like?" Alex asked, suddenly curious.

Love mixed with embarrassment reflected back at him. "Don't ask."

His heart went out to her and he wished he'd kept his mouth shut. Having parents you couldn't look up to had to be hard. Though Alex hadn't always agreed with every decision his parents made, they were honorable people. No wonder Lauren wasn't eager to talk about her mother and father.

Still, he sensed the last thing she'd want was his pity.

"Sara has a beautiful voice." Alex cupped her elbow in his hand and guided her through the thinning crowd lingering in front of the church. "I'm glad you insisted I come with you."

"*I* insisted?" The tiny lines between Lauren's eyebrows eased and she smiled.

He grinned. "Maybe I remembered incorrectly."

"Maybe you did." Lauren chuckled and let him take her arm.

She had a sneaking suspicion Alex had deliberately changed the subject and she found his gallantry touching. Maybe having him as a roommate was going to work out after all.

"Let's go to lunch," Alex said unexpectedly. "You pick the place."

Lauren hesitated. The rent money he'd given her last night was already spoken for. So, unless he was picking up the tab, she couldn't afford even a flavored toothpick. But if she let him pay, it would seem like a date. And tempted though she might be, she knew that the only way the two of them living under the same roof was going to work was if they kept their relationship strictly business.

A fleeting image of the Grotto's fettuccine Alfredo flashed before her. She could almost taste the creamy sauce and homemade noodles. Her stomach growled loudly offering its input. "I'm not hungry."

His eyes widened then narrowed.

"I understand." But the tiny muscle tightening along his jawline told Lauren he didn't understand at all.

He thought she didn't want to go out with *him*. This, unfortunately, was not the case. The simple fact was, if she had money she'd go. But she didn't. And the only thing worse than being broke was being someone's charity case.

And that, she refused to be.

Alex wheeled the Buick into the driveway and heaved an exhausted sigh. He'd started the day at six and hadn't slowed down since, not even for lunch. That's why when his colleagues had asked him to join them for dinner—despite an empty wallet— he'd been seriously tempted.

But his recent layoff had depleted most of his savings, and he had to get them built up again. He still had five months to get through and he had to be prepared in case something went wrong. Ramen noodles for dinner would have to be enough.

Strangely, the thought didn't bother him. In the last six months his ability to eat on a pittance had become a source of pride. It was a far different life than what he'd been used to. Henri, the royal chef had been Cordon Bleu trained and every meal had been a culinary masterpiece.

Alex realized now that he'd taken Henri and all that fabulous food for granted. He couldn't remember the last time he'd bothered to compliment Henri on a job well done.

The thought gave him pause. Perhaps some good had come from this year. When his mother had first announced the ridiculous contest of sorts, Alex had decided she was just being punitive. He'd been convinced she hadn't picked him as her successor because she was angry over him skipping a royal function to attend the World Boating Championships in Monte Carlo. Of course, it didn't help that the bill had just arrived for an impromptu party he'd thrown in Paris the week before, the final cost of which had stunned even him.

Regardless of the reason, Alex was now in the position where he had to prove himself. But thanks to meeting Lauren, getting through these last few months was going to be far easier than he'd imagined.

The soft light from the living room lamps cast a welcoming glow and anticipation quickened Alex's step. Though money *had* been a factor, deep down Alex knew part of the reason he'd said no to dinner was because he liked coming home. He liked telling Lauren about his day and hearing about hers. Rushing off to a noisy restaurant held little appeal.

It was crazy when he thought about it; he, Alexander Gabrielle, Prince of Carpegnia, turning down an invitation so he could stay *home*.

His friends would laugh their heads off if they heard. Just like he'd laughed when they'd announced they were getting married and settling down. And when he'd stopped laughing, he'd told them they were insane to give up their freewheeling bachelor ways for domesticity.

It had made no sense to him. But now, for the first time, Alex was able to understand a little of what drove his friends to embrace a more traditional lifestyle.

He pushed open the front door and stopped, inhaling the aroma of freshly baked cookies. Was it any wonder he loved his new home? He smiled and headed straight for the kitchen.

Lauren stood by the oven, a spatula in hand. She turned at his footsteps. "You're home early."

Alex liked the way the word *home* sounded on her lips. He took a step closer to the stove and the light, airy fragrance that he'd come to associate with Lauren teased his nostrils.

His body stirred. "Something smells good in here."

Lauren made a wide, sweeping arc with one hand, gesturing to the golden-brown morsels cooling on the table. "The children are bringing their grandparents to school tomorrow and we're having punch and cookies."

Alex took a step closer. "It's not the cookies."

She tilted her head and confusion filled her gaze. "Then what?"

"You." He now stood so close he could see her pulse fluttering in her neck. "You smell absolutely delicious."

Lauren's eyes darkened momentarily before she chuckled. "One of my students told me that I smelled good enough to eat."

"I agree." Alex reached for her, then stopped and sniffed. "Is something burning?"

Lauren whirled. She gasped at the sight of smoke rising from the skillet. Without hesitation, she grabbed the handle and lifted it off the burner.

"That was a close call," she said, exhaling a breath. "Thanks for the warning."

"What was it supposed to be?" Alex leaned over her shoulder, his gaze settling on the charred bread. "Grilled cheese?"

"That was last night." Lauren flipped on the vent fan with well-practiced ease. "Tonight I was aiming for something a little more exotic."

Alex shifted his gaze back to the bread. Whatever it had been was burned beyond recognition. "Give me a clue."

She shook her head and her lips quirked upward. "I might as well tell you because you'll never guess. It was a grilled peanut-butter sandwich."

"I've never heard of such a thing." Not only had Alex never heard of it, he had the feeling Henri would be horrified that such a sandwich existed.

"You haven't lived until you've had one," Lauren said. "Couple it with some fruit and a glass of milk and you have all the food groups."

"Is that so?" Alex said cautiously, not knowing what else to say.

"Want to try it?"

Alex paused. A hot sandwich—however strange—sounded better than ramen noodles. But the glint in Lauren's eye told him she was up to something. "What's the catch?"

"No catch." Lauren smiled innocently. "Of course, after we eat if you'd like to help me with the dishes, I wouldn't say no."

His gaze slid to the sink filled with bowls and spoons and flat metal sheets. "I thought that was what dishwashers were for?"

Lauren wrinkled her nose. "It's on the fritz. The repair place wanted a hundred dollars just to look at it. So if you'd like to help…"

Alex stared down at his hands. A prince doing dishes? Impossible.

"How about if I throw in a couple of cookies?" Lauren asked with a hopeful smile. "Chocolate goes great with peanut butter."

He wanted to say "add a kiss and it's a deal" but

he stopped himself just in time. Lauren had made it extremely clear when he'd moved in what her expectations were and he wasn't about to rock the boat. He liked living here too much to risk being thrown out on the street.

"They've got pecans in them."

Now she sounded almost desperate.

For the first time Alex noticed the lines of fatigue edging her eyes and he realized he wasn't the only one who'd had a long, tiring day. After dinner, she'd still have papers to grade and lesson plans to prepare.

Alex glanced at the sink.

A prince doing dishes?

He smiled. "It's a deal."

By the end of the week, things had settled into a routine. In the mornings, Lauren would come downstairs and Alex would be in the kitchen with a cup of coffee ready for her.

Over toast and cereal they'd discuss their plans for the day before heading off to their respective jobs. He usually got home after she did, but more often than not they ended up eating together in the evening, too. Alex had given her extra money for groceries and Lauren figured as long as she was making one sandwich, she might as well make two.

Tonight she'd decided to go all out. A friend had

given her a recipe for chicken enchiladas, but she'd never been able to justify going to all the work of making them for just one person. But now she had Alex.

The salad was chilling in the refrigerator, the enchiladas simmering on the stove, when Lauren heard the front door open.

"Where's that beautiful roommate of mine?"

Her heart flip-flopped in her chest and for one crazy second, Lauren had an overpowering urge to fling the silverware on the table, run to the door and throw her arms around his neck.

She chalked up the insane urge to frustration. Ever since he'd moved in, Alex had been a perfect gentleman. It was what she'd told him she wanted, what she'd insisted he agree to, before he moved into her home. But lately she'd been having second thoughts. What would be so wrong with a kiss on the cheek now and then? And if her mouth happened to find his, would it really be such a big deal?

The more she thought about it, the more her heart skittered in his presence and the more her lips longed for his. It was obvious she'd been too hard-nosed. But how to let him know she'd changed her mind?

"Somebody's been cooking again." Alex stopped in the doorway and sniffed the air. "And it smells wonderful."

He looked so incredibly handsome in his navy

sweater and pants that Lauren made herself lower her gaze so he wouldn't see the desire flickering in the depths.

"Chicken enchiladas," she said. "I've got more than enough, so if you're hungry—"

"Actually I just came home to change," he said.

"To change?" Lauren tilted her head. Either the heat from the stove had affected her brain or he wasn't making any sense. "You have to work tonight?"

"Not work. Play." He popped an olive from the relish tray into his mouth and flashed a boyish smile. "I have a date."

His words hit hard, like a one-two punch straight to the gut. She hadn't realized Alex even knew any other women in St. Louis. To her horror, Lauren found herself blinking back tears.

Thankfully, Alex was busy surveying the table and didn't seem to notice.

"I should have called and told you I wouldn't be home for dinner," he said, sincere regret in his tone.

"No problem." Somehow her voice came out clear and steady. "I hadn't really counted on you being here anyway."

He moved closer but instead of looking up, Lauren kept her gaze focused on the table. She straightened the place mats and adjusted napkin rings, hoping he wouldn't be perceptive enough to see that her actions were completely unnecessary.

"Then why the two place settings?" he asked in a low tone.

For a second she was tempted to tell him the truth, but it was the note of sympathy in his voice that changed her mind. Lauren Carlyle didn't need any man's pity.

She took a deep breath, met his gaze and lied through her teeth. "Rusty is coming over. He was going to take me out but I'd wanted to make this recipe for ages so I told him we could just eat here."

Though she could have said more to increase the story's believability, Lauren shut her mouth. She had a tendency to chatter when she was nervous and she told herself it was best to stop while she was ahead.

"I could change my plans…." The concerned look in his eyes told her he still had some doubts.

"Why would you do that?" Lauren forced a laugh. "Go. Have fun with your new friends."

She sensed, rather than saw, him relax.

"Rusty seems like a nice guy," he said conversationally.

"He is," Lauren agreed, wishing desperately that Alex didn't feel the need to stay and talk.

"It was apparent to me the other night," Alex continued, "that he really likes you."

Lauren resisted the urge to sigh. Instead she attempted a weak smile before turning back to the table.

"I'd better shower," Alex said, but he made no move to leave.

"Yes, you'd better." The lump in Lauren's throat made it difficult for her to breathe, much less talk, but she did her best to force a light tone. "Wouldn't want to keep the new girlfriend waiting."

"She's not my girlfriend." Alex stood behind her now, so close she could feel his warm breath against the back of her neck. "And if you want to know the truth, *she* asked *me* if I wanted to go with her and some friends for dinner and a few drinks. I didn't ask her."

Lauren didn't care who asked whom, only that he'd agreed to go. That meant he had to be somewhat interested in this woman. Though she didn't want to prolong the conversation, some type of comment seemed warranted. "How did you two meet?"

"Carly works for the travel agency handling the reservations for Sara's tour," he said.

"Carly." Lauren tried not to grimace. "What a pretty name."

"I guess," he said. "Listen, Lauren. I—"

"I'd love to talk more about your new girlfriend, Alex. But I'm afraid—"

"How many times do I have to tell you, she's not my new girlfriend." Alex spoke between gritted teeth. "We're just going to dinner."

"And you'll have a wonderful time." How Lauren

managed to say the words so sincerely she wasn't sure. "But, as I was saying, Rusty is going to be here shortly and I haven't even started to get ready."

"You don't need to do a thing." Alex's gaze lingered on the simple dress pants and white cashmere top she'd worn to school. "You look beautiful just the way you are."

Though the compliment warmed her heart, Lauren knew he was only being kind. The outfit was more serviceable than trendy.

Carly would probably wear a dress tonight. Maybe one of those cute little numbers that Lauren had admired on a Nordstrom mannequin just last week.

A perfect dress for a perfect date.

Lauren's heart clenched but she somehow managed to smile.

"Save the compliments for Carly," Lauren said. "No need to waste them on me."

Chapter Eight

Alex glanced at his watch, glad he'd met Carly at the restaurant instead of picking her up. Driving separately made it easier to make a clean exit.

Not that he hadn't enjoyed the evening. Carly was a perky blonde with an outgoing personality. It would be hard *not* to like her. Her friends were nice and the dinner and conversation had been enjoyable.

But from the moment he'd come home from work and had seen Lauren, Alex had wondered what madness had possessed him to agree to this evening out. He'd wanted nothing more than to cancel his plans and spend the evening with her. Until she'd mentioned Rusty.

Alex still wasn't sure if the guy had been an excuse or if he really was coming over. It had been that doubt that had made him decide to go out. After all, if she and Rusty had a romantic evening planned…

His hand tightened around the stem of his wineglass. Rusty seemed liked an okay guy, but he wasn't the right man for Lauren. Seeing the two together at Sara's house had told Alex that much.

"Do you have one?"

Alex blinked and focused his gaze on Carly and her friend, Aimee. The rest of the group had scattered, leaving only the three of them. Aimee had been living in California the past five years and was in the process of moving back to St. Louis. Carly hadn't even known her friend was back until she'd unexpectedly shown up at the restaurant.

Though Carly had done her best during the course of the evening to include Alex in the conversation, she and her old friend had a lot of catching up to do. Alex hadn't minded. The wives of the two other men had talked nonstop with each other while the men had discussed sports. By throwing in a few comments every now and then, Alex had been able to be a part of their conversation with very little effort.

But after they'd left, he'd gotten lost in his own thoughts and right now he didn't have a clue what Carly had asked him. "Have what?"

Carly cast a sideways smile at her friend. "I knew he wasn't listening."

Aimee took a sip of her wine and gazed up at Alex through lowered lashes. "We were talking about brothers. Carly asked if you had one?"

"Actually I have two," Alex said. His voice warmed as it always did when he thought of his younger brothers. Though they'd fought like the devil while growing up—and still did at times—he'd do anything for them.

Aimee's eyes brightened with interest. "Do they live close?"

Alex shook his head. "Luc lives in Boston. Gabe is up in Montana."

"Do you see them often?" Carly asked.

"Not as often as I'd like," Alex admitted. He'd talked with them quite a bit the first couple of months he'd been in the United States, but it had been at least six weeks since he'd spoken with any of his family. "You know how it is, life gets in the way."

Carly nodded in agreement.

"I am so bummed." Aimee heaved a melodramatic sigh. "Carly and I were just talking about how great it would be if you had a brother in town. That way the four of us could double-date."

Alex offered a noncommittal smile. Though he'd enjoyed the evening, he didn't plan on seeing Carly again. At least, not socially. His time in St. Louis was limited and when he'd walked out the door tonight, he'd decided that if he had any extra moments, he wanted to spend them with Lauren.

He wondered if she'd still be up when he got home.

More importantly, would Rusty be there with her?

Alex pressed his lips together as an image of Lauren in the other man's arms flashed before him.

"Alex?"

His head jerked up and for a second Alex could only stare. It was as if the mere thought of Lauren's old friend had conjured him up.

"What a surprise." Alex stood and glanced around, surprised to discover that Rusty appeared to be alone. "I didn't think I'd see you this evening."

"That makes two of us." The man grinned, but didn't elaborate. His gaze slid curiously to the two women at the table.

Alex quickly performed the introductions, noticing that Rusty held Aimee's hand for an extra beat. He found it particularly noteworthy considering the fact that Rusty had to have just left Lauren.

"Would you like to join us?" Alex asked. He made the offer more out of politeness than any real desire to spend time with the man.

Rusty's gaze settled on the petite dark-haired Aimee. "Don't mind if I do."

The words to ask about Lauren were already on

Alex's lips when he reined them in. Though he was intensely curious why she wasn't with Rusty, he'd learned long ago that it was decidedly bad form to ask about one woman when you were with another.

Carly nudged Alex with her elbow. "He might not be a brother, but he'll do."

Her tone was low and clearly meant for Alex's ears only. But listening to Rusty and Aimee's laughter, Alex realized Carly could have spoken in her normal voice and the two wouldn't have heard.

As happy as Alex was to see Rusty paying attention to a woman other than Lauren, he couldn't help but think the guy a fool.

"Rusty and my landlord are old friends," Alex said to Carly. Though in some ways the comment might appear to come out of the blue, it not only explained how he and Rusty knew each other, it gave Alex the opportunity to bring up Lauren without being obvious.

Rusty's gaze shifted from the woman to Alex.

"Lauren and I have known each other since high school," Rusty explained, shooting Aimee a reassuring smile. "How is she, by the way?"

"Don't you know?" Alex asked.

Rusty shook his head. "Haven't seen her since last week at Sara's house."

There was no guile in Rusty's eyes and Alex suddenly realized that Lauren had lied. But that was between him and Lauren, not anyone else. Alex kept his expression carefully controlled. "Has it been that long?"

"Long?" Carly laughed. "I have friends who live here in town I haven't seen since Christmas. Like you were saying, sometimes life gets crazy and before you know it months have gone by."

Rusty's gaze slid to Aimee. "I've always believed we make time for what's important."

Alex rose to his feet. This time he had to agree with Rusty.

It *was* time.

Time Alex went home.

And time he focused on what was important.

Ever since Alex had walked out the door earlier in the evening, Lauren's stomach had been upset. The chicken enchiladas had turned out perfectly, but Lauren hadn't been able to eat a bite. Just staring down at the sauce had been enough to make her gag.

She couldn't afford to be sick and she hoped whatever she was coming down with didn't last long. It was already April and she had a lot still to teach her kindergartners before the end of the year. Even one day of missed work would throw her off schedule. Unfortunately, being exposed to germs was a daily occupational hazard.

Lauren took a deep breath and willed her stomach to settle down. The food was all put away, so thankfully she didn't have to see or smell it. She tried to relax and watch television but she couldn't handle the commercials. Not to mention it was hard to concentrate on some silly sitcom when Alex was out on a *date*.

So she shut off the set, changed out of her work clothes and settled into a soft oversized chair with a book. Though it was only ten-thirty, her eyelids started to droop…until she heard the key in the lock.

Instantly she was wide awake. She'd never expected Alex home this early.

The front door creaked open, then thudded shut. Alex's footsteps echoed as he moved through the silent house.

Earlier in the evening Lauren had pulled her hair into a stubby ponytail, scrubbed her face free of makeup and put on her pajamas. Then she'd wrapped herself up in the chenille robe her grandmother had given her before she died. Though it wasn't particularly stylish, Lauren loved the robe. When she pulled it on she could almost feel her grandmother's comforting embrace.

"Lauren?" Alex called out.

Lauren glanced at the staircase. Though he was closing in, she still had time to make her escape. After all, she'd have to be crazy to let any man, much less the handsome hunk she lived with, see her looking like Frieda Frump.

But she didn't feel like racing up the steps. Besides, what did it matter anyway? The man had a girlfriend. One who probably always looked perfectly put together. Why, it wouldn't even surprise her if *Carly* could afford to shop at Nordstrom even when they weren't having a sale.

Unexpected tears filled her eyes and this time she didn't even try to push them away.

"Lauren?" Alex stood in the doorway. Even though mistiness clouded her vision, she could see the concern in his eyes. "Why are you crying?"

She lifted her shoulders in a helpless shrug. How could she explain something she didn't understand herself?

He quickly crossed the room and squatted down in front of her. "What's wrong?"

Lauren wiped away the tears that had been coming with increasing frequency the past week and sniffed. "I just feel funky."

"You seemed okay when I left."

The worry in his eyes warmed her heart and for a second all she could do was stare.

"I *was* okay," she said, finally finding her voice. "But that's how this bug operates. One minute you're okay, the next it hits you."

He laid the back of his hand across her forehead. "You don't feel like you have a fever."

"It's my stomach," she said with a wobbly

smile. "I couldn't even eat the nice dinner I cooked."

"Oh, Lauren..."

The tenderness in his gaze almost did her in. If she didn't get a grip, she'd be blubbering all over the front of his shirt.

"You better get away," she said. "We had two teachers out last week. I don't want you to catch this."

"Don't worry about me." Alex gently brushed a strand of hair back from her forehead with the tips of his fingers. "I'm rarely sick. In fact, the entire time I was growing up, I bet the doctor only came to see me two or three times."

Lauren shivered beneath his touch and wondered if she had a fever that was affecting her hearing. "The doctor came to your house? You didn't have to go to the office?"

Alex smiled. "That's the way things work in Carpegnia."

Lauren sighed. "Sounds nice."

"It is," Alex said in a nostalgic tone. "There's no better place on earth."

Lauren laid the book that was resting in her lap on the side table, her upset stomach forgotten. "If you like it so much, why did you move halfway across the world?"

"It's a long story."

"I'd like to hear it." Though moments before Lauren had been dozing, Alex's presence had energized her. Right now she didn't feel the least bit tired or sick. "Talking might take my mind off how I feel."

Lauren had been curious about Alex's background since they'd met and she hoped he'd give her more pieces of the puzzle. So many things about him didn't add up. He had expensive clothes but a beater of a car. He clearly appreciated the finer things in life, but hoarded his money.

"I wouldn't want to keep you up." Alex's gaze slid from her face to the faded blue robe. "You look like you're ready for bed."

Though there was no judgment in his observation, Lauren flushed with embarrassment. "I was just relaxing."

"Rusty must have gone home early."

Now her cheeks weren't just warm, they were red hot. When she'd told him Rusty was coming over, Lauren had justified the falsehood by telling herself it was no big deal, a little white lie to preserve her dignity and keep Alex from feeling uncomfortable.

Lying was something that had always been acceptable in the Carlyle household and, though she hated to admit it, lying came more naturally to Lauren than telling the truth. But staring into his eyes, she knew she had to come clean.

"Rusty never came over." Lauren's heart started

thumping in her chest and her palms began to sweat but she tightened her resolve and forged ahead. "There never were any plans for him to come over."

"Then why—?"

"The dinner was for you." Lauren forced herself to meet his gaze. After all, she reminded herself, she'd gone out of her way to be nice and that was a good thing. "I knew you had to be tired of sandwiches and soup and I wanted to make something special."

His eyes softened. "Why didn't you tell me?"

For a second Lauren was tempted to say that when he'd told her he had a date, she hadn't wanted to make him feel obligated. But that was only part of it, and this conversation was about being honest.

"I was embarrassed." She shifted her gaze to her hands. "I didn't want you to know I'd done it for you."

"Oh, Lauren."

In less than a heartbeat, Alex's arms were around her and his mouth was on hers. His lips were warm and soft and the kiss slow and leisurely. The strength of his arms and gentleness of his touch brought back the memories of their night together. Tears filled her eyes and she drew him close. He'd been a wonderful lover.

They continued to kiss and without realizing quite how it happened, Lauren found herself next to him on the floor, his lips still pressed against hers.

His hand slid inside the collar of her robe and stroked her skin.

Logic told her she should put some distance between them but instead she found herself reciprocating, stroking the back of his neck, twining her fingers in his thick, soft hair. They hadn't been this close since the night in the hotel.

Alex's tongue teased the fullness of her lower lip, coaxing her to open to him, sweeping inside when she did. He tasted of wine and spearmint, a ridiculous combination that suddenly seemed almost erotic.

Lauren splayed her fingers against the fabric of his shirt and leaned into the kiss, her tongue fencing with his until the delicious thrust and slide had her pulse hammering in her veins and something tightening low in her belly.

His fingers loosened the belt of her robe but, lost in a spinning whirl of desire, Lauren barely noticed. Only when his hand rose to her breast did she realize the danger.

Though she wanted nothing more than to throw caution to the winds and beg him to make love to her, Lauren knew she'd regret following her heart. Dazed and breathing hard, she pushed his hands away and clutched the robe closed with trembling fingers.

"We can't do this." Her breath came in short puffs, and her voice sounded raspy and harsh even to her own ears.

"Why not?" His gaze reflected the same heat, the same unbidden hunger that coursed through her.

"I can't...." Despite Lauren's best intentions, her voice came out high and shaky. "When you leave..."

She bit her lip and struggled to gain control of her emotions.

"It would just be too hard," Lauren said finally.

Despite her words, she found herself wishing that he would take her in his arms and kiss her doubts away. Promise her he'd never leave. Do or say whatever it took to get her back in his arms.

But he remained silent. Instead, after a long moment, he rose to his feet, and held out a hand to her. "Of course. I respect your decision."

His touch sent a shiver up her spine and she wished with all her heart it could be different. But while some women could handle casual sex, she wasn't one of them.

"I do understand," he said gently when she didn't speak. "Though I think we could have had a good time tonight."

Lauren didn't know whether to laugh or cry. All she knew at the moment was the guy definitely had a talent for understatement.

Chapter Nine

"Thanks for making the cocoa." Lauren leaned back in the chair and took a cautious sip of the steaming chocolate. "It's wonderful."

"I'm glad you like it." Alex had been waited on all his life and it felt surprisingly good to wait on someone else for a change.

Lauren took another sip. "It's weird but my stomach feels fine now. Maybe I'm not getting sick after all."

Alex stirred the marshmallows into his drink with the tip of his spoon and hid a smile. He could have told her she wasn't sick. Lauren could be rather high-strung and he'd had the feeling all along that her jumpy stomach resulted from her dinner plans going awry. Someone who was sick could never have responded to his kisses the way she had. His body tightened, remembering the taste of her lips, the feel of her soft skin beneath his hand….

"Tell me about your evening." Lauren wrapped her fingers around the mug. "How was your date?"

Her words were like a splash of cold water. Date? There were thousands of things they could discuss and she wanted to talk about another woman?

"It was okay," Alex said with a shrug. The evening was a nonevent as far as he was concerned. Four wasted hours that he could have spent at home.

"Just okay?" Lauren prompted.

Alex hesitated for a moment. When he did speak, he chose his words carefully, not wanting to disparage Carly or the others in any way.

"Carly is a nice woman. Her friends are nice. There's nothing wrong with her or them. But I don't plan on seeing her again. At least not socially."

Surprise skittered across Lauren's face. "Why is that?"

It seemed a ridiculous question for her to ask after what had happened between them less than a half hour before, but she appeared to expect an answer.

"I'll be leaving soon," he said finally. "I'm not interested in a serious relationship and she made it clear that's what she's looking for."

Lauren licked the stickiness off her spoon. "Did you tell her that?"

His brows pulled together. "We went out one time."

"And you had fun."

"Yes, but—"

"She's probably expecting you to call."

"I didn't say I would." Alex narrowed his gaze. "Why are you trying to push her on me, anyway?"

"I'm not," Lauren said. "I just know how it feels to be on her end."

The pain in her voice quelled his anger and reminded him how different Lauren was from other women he'd dated. They'd be more likely to claw a competitor's eyes out than to sympathize with them.

"And how is that?" he asked quietly.

"You go out with a guy. You have a good time. He seems to enjoy your company, too. The evening ends and your expectation is that he'll call and ask you out again." She paused for a moment and her lips twisted in a humorless smile. "But he doesn't. You blame yourself. Maybe I shouldn't have said this. Maybe I should have said that. Maybe I talked too much. Maybe I didn't talk enough. It can drive you crazy."

"So you're telling me I should have said point blank at the end of the evening I wouldn't be calling?"

"Yes. No." Lauren heaved a sigh. "I don't know. I just feel sorry for her. Women always get the short end of the stick."

"Not always."

"Yes, they do," Lauren insisted. "I bet you can't give me even one example where a guy you know got dumped on."

Alex thought about his friend's wedding just last summer. "My friend Harry is a great example."

Lauren sipped her cocoa and didn't comment, but the look in her eyes told him she was listening.

"He met this woman on a business trip. Though he is usually very sensible, from the moment he saw her he was convinced she was the one for him."

Lauren leaned forward, rested the cup on the table and smiled. "How romantic. Love at first sight."

Alex resisted the urge to snort.

"Initially the attraction was all one-sided. Then she did a complete about-face. Harry was well known in certain social circles and the only thing I can figure is she must have found out how much he was worth." Alex's lips twisted. He'd always hated gold-diggers. "Suddenly she was all too eager to get 'better acquainted.' The next time I saw him, she was pregnant. Apparently she'd conveniently 'forgotten' to take a couple of her birth control pills one month."

Lauren's eyes widened. "What happened?"

"What do you think?" Alex couldn't believe she had to ask. "Harry is an honorable man. He married her."

"Are they happy?"

Alex shrugged. "I doubt it."

"How sad," Lauren said. "For him. And for her."

"For her?" Alex couldn't believe his ears. "She has everything."

"Not everything," Lauren said. "She doesn't have a man who loves her and who truly wants to be with her. And if you don't have that, you don't have anything."

If you don't have someone who loves you and wants to be with you, you don't have anything.

At work the next day, Alex found himself mulling Lauren's words. His mother had said virtually the same thing when he'd insisted that bringing Carpegnia into the twenty-first century fiscally strong had to be her greatest accomplishment. She'd smiled and said that while that brought her much pride and satisfaction, it was her husband and children who gave life meaning.

His mother had made no secret of the fact that she wanted him to have the same happiness in his life. But even if he were inclined to marry, that wasn't going to happen for a while. His entire focus had to be on the task at hand.

Alex couldn't quite still the bitterness that welled up inside him. He'd counted on being appointed his mother's successor, not just because he was the oldest, but because he was the best choice. His brother Gabe loved living in Paris and rarely made it home and his youngest brother, Luc, was more interested in seeing the world than in ruling Carpegnia.

But instead of bestowing the Sacred Sword of Carpegnia upon the only clear choice, his mother had announced she was having difficulty choosing between her sons and would postpone her decision for a year.

He remembered that afternoon as if it were yesterday….

Alex shut and locked the library door firmly behind him, ensuring that he and his mother wouldn't be interrupted. It had been chaotic in the palace ever since his mother had announced she would reign for another year.

"You're upset," she said quietly. But her gaze was strong and steady and there wasn't a hint of apology in her tone.

"I deserved to be chosen." The anger and humiliation that had been building up inside Alex since that morning exploded. "You know that as well as I do."

His mother's gaze narrowed at his abrupt tone but she didn't call him on it. "I never meant to hurt or embarrass you. But, at this point, I'm not convinced you *are* the best one to rule Carpegnia."

"You can't actually believe Gabe or Luc would make a better king?" Disbelief rang in Alex's voice.

"You each have your own strengths and weaknesses," she said. "It's important I make the right decision."

"Is this because I skipped that boring summit on natural resources? Or was it that party I threw last month in Paris? I admit the charges were a bit excessive—"

"Alex. That's the past. This upcoming year is about the future." She leaned forward and rested her hand flat against his face. "Prove to me—and to yourself—that you are the most worthy."

"Alex?"

The unexpected voice jerked Alex back to the present. He blinked and looked up. Sal stood in the open doorway.

"Got a minute?"

Alex gestured to the only other chair in his makeshift office. "Have a seat."

"Thanks." Sal plopped into the chair. "Did you resolve that double booking problem?"

Alex tilted his head. Until now, Sal had stayed in the background of Sara's tour plans. The only parts that had concerned him were related to security issues. And Alex had the feeling that's the way the man wanted it. That's why this sudden interest didn't make sense. "You didn't stop by to talk about that."

"You're right," Sal laughed. "I didn't."

Alex leaned back in his chair and waited for Sal to explain.

Sal cast Alex a speculative look. "Sara mentioned you and Lauren have been spending a lot of time together."

"We live under the same roof," Alex said. "Spending time together goes with the territory."

"Have you told her you're a prince?"

Alex shook his head. Ever since Sal had mentioned he'd had him investigated, Alex had wondered when this would come up.

"When I first met Sara, I conveniently forgot to mention I was a cop hired to protect her. That was a mistake." Sal shook his head. "I learned the hard way that women hate lies."

"Does Sara know my background?"

"I didn't want to say anything to her until I'd had a chance to talk to you," Sal said. "I just can't figure out why the big secret? And why *are* you in St. Louis working for my wife? It's not like you need the money."

"It's complicated," Alex said, remembering the promise they'd all made not to trade on their royal status.

Sal leaned back in the chair. "I'm not in any hurry."

Not only wasn't Sal in any hurry, when the former cop put his feet up on the desk Alex knew Sal wasn't planning to leave anytime soon.

Alex sighed. Though he wasn't eager to tell the

story, in some ways it would be a relief to come clean with Sal. He'd always hated lying to friends and he considered his employer's husband a friend.

"It has to do with succession," Alex said. "In many countries, the crown goes to the firstborn son. That's not the case where I come from. If it were, I'd already be king."

Sal's gaze was intent, but he didn't say a word.

"In Carpegnia, the reigning monarch chooses a successor when their youngest child turns twenty-five," Alex continued. "Last year my youngest brother had his twenty-fifth birthday. But instead of announcing her successor, my mother decided to wait a year before bestowing the Sacred Sword of Carpegnia."

"Sacred Sword?"

Alex smiled at the confusion on Sal's face. It was easy to forget that not everyone was familiar with his country's traditions. "The Sacred Sword is embedded with the crown jewels and it is bestowed upon the successor in a special ceremony. The passing of the sword is symbolic of the passing of power."

"So your mother rules another year," Sal said as if it were no big deal. "And you hang out."

"It's a little more complicated than that," Alex said. "She gave me and each of my brothers ten thousand dollars and a year in America to prove ourselves worthy. At the end of this year, she'll look at how we've done and choose her successor."

If Alex knew for certain his mother could choose him, he wouldn't mind waiting this year. But she could just as easily decide to pick one of his brothers.

Sal's gaze turned sharp and assessing. "Do you think you'll be the 'chosen one'?"

Alex sighed. "At this point I have no idea."

His mother was deeply committed to protecting her country's resources. And he knew she had concerns about his spending habits and his lifestyle. That's why Alex had decided the best way to show her he'd changed would be to spend this year living within his means. He'd only spend what he made and, at the end of the summer, he'd return the entire ten thousand dollars to her.

But would it be enough? He hoped so.

Because his entire future depended on it.

Chapter Ten

Lauren rested her chin on her hand and stared down at the bills littering the dining room table. Another payday and nothing had changed. It didn't take a mathematical genius to figure out there wasn't going to be any money left for shopping. The thought was too depressing for words. All week she'd looked forward to picking up some new spring clothes at the Galleria.

Lately she'd been as jumpy as a cat. Any little thing made her cry and minor irritations took on major importance. And now she couldn't even go on a shopping spree....

The front door slammed shut and Lauren's melancholy mood vanished. Seeing Alex always brightened her spirits. It was amazing. They'd lived under the same roof for almost five weeks and were still on friendly terms.

Very friendly terms.

Ever since Alex had discovered she wasn't going to throw him out for showing affection, Lauren had seen a whole different side to him. She'd discovered that Alex Gabrielle was a demonstrative guy. He was always taking her hand, putting his arm around her shoulders or giving her a quick hug. She could handle the affectionate gestures, but it was the passionate kisses that threw her off balance and kept her awake at night.

"Hey, beautiful." The object of her nighttime fantasies strode into the room and planted a kiss on the top of her head. "Why so glum?"

Lauren gestured with one hand to the bills. "Need I say more?"

"Don't tell me the wolf is howling at the door?" His tone was teasing and a hint of a smile tugged at the corners of his lips.

"Not quite that bad." Lauren had to admit that Alex's rent money had been a godsend. Instead of losing ground every month, she was now at least able to keep up. But that was little consolation.

She heaved a heavy sigh. "There's no money left for shopping and I really wanted to check out the new spring things."

Alex plopped down in the chair next to hers.

"Nothing says you can't look. Last I knew that didn't cost anything."

It sounded so simple. Unfortunately, the reality was a little more complicated. The last time Lauren had tried window shopping she'd come home with three bags of clothes she'd had to return.

"If I look I'll want to buy," she said. "And I *will* buy, even if I don't have the money. That's why I have to stay away. But I really need to go. Does that make sense?"

Alex grinned. "No."

Lauren thought she'd been extremely clear, but she reminded herself that he was a man and his brain worked differently. She'd have to spell it out. "In case you haven't noticed, I've been feeling kind of stressed this week."

Though she'd snapped at him a couple of times in the past few days, Alex apparently had been around women enough to know he'd be a fool to agree. "What does that have to do with shopping?"

"This may sound crazy to you, but walking down the aisles, studying the displays and feeling the fabric relaxes me." A dreamy smile lifted her lips. "It's even better than chocolate."

"But you can't go without wanting to buy," Alex said, appearing to finally get the point. "Spending money you don't have makes you stressed. So it's a catch-22."

"Exactly." Lauren said.

"I've got a suggestion," Alex said. "It works for me when I'm feeling stressed so it may work for you."

"When do *you* ever feel stressed?" Lauren asked. She'd never met a guy more even-natured. "For that matter, what do you even have to feel stressed about?"

He smiled even as his eyes took on a faraway look. "You'd be surprised."

Lauren tilted her head. She was starting to realize there was still so much about this man she didn't know. "Okay, share. What's the miracle cure?"

"Running," he said.

Lauren groaned. "I'm on my feet all day at school."

"It's not the same." Alex reached down, grabbed her hand and pulled her to her feet. "I've discovered this trail down by Forest Park that I know you'll love."

"I'll collapse after five minutes," Lauren said.

"Don't worry," Alex leaned close and his breath tickled her ear, "I know CPR."

Her knees went weak and, though she hadn't yet taken a step, Lauren could almost feel a swoon coming on. "I'll bet you do."

"You don't believe me?" He wiggled his eyebrow melodramatically. "Maybe we should have ourselves a little practice session?"

"Maybe we should," Lauren said, calling his bluff.

Alex smiled smugly and she had the feeling she'd played right into his hands. Or, maybe he'd played right into hers.

It started out as a simple kiss, if there ever was such a thing between the two of them. But when her lips parted and he claimed her mouth, a wave of heat washed through her.

So familiar. Alex's hand came up to cradle the back of her head and he shifted the angle of the kiss, deepening it. His tongue stroked her mouth in a blatantly carnal rhythm that made something tighten in the pit of her stomach and dissolved the remaining strength in her knees.

So overwhelming. Lauren struggled to draw a breath as he scattered kisses along her neck. It was too much. Too much heat. Too much hunger. Too much need.

The feel of him, the taste of him consumed her. His hand flattened against her lower back, drawing her up against the length of his body and her hips arched in instinctive invitation.

"I want to make to love to you," he whispered against her throat.

She wanted that, too. But the barriers that had kept her from giving in to her desires before still existed and couldn't be ignored.

"We can't," Lauren whispered shakily.

"Why not?" Alex trailed his tongue along the scooped neck of her shirt and for a second Lauren not only forgot how to think, but how to breathe.

When his hand rose and he started to tug the shirt lower, Lauren's hand closed over his with a firmness that surprised even her. "I can't handle a fling."

In this day of fast and easy sex, the words sounded ridiculous. But it was the truth. Lauren was scared to death of the way he made her feel; of the heat that could flare so quickly between them, but most of all of the increasing need she had for him.

She couldn't let herself get any closer. Already she found herself caring far too much about someone who, in a matter of a few short months, would be gone.

No, she had to stay the course and maintain some distance between them. Because the last thing she needed as a souvenir of their time together was a broken heart.

The Missouri sky was a vivid blue and Lauren had never seen Forest Park look more beautiful. If she could only stop and smell the flowers…

Though Alex didn't even appear winded from their jog, Lauren was convinced her lungs were mere seconds away from exploding. That was assuming, of course, that her legs didn't give out first.

It surprised her that she was this out of shape. Though she wasn't a gym rat, she was a yoga addict and she walked miles every day in her classroom. But lately she'd been so exhausted that by the end of the day all she wanted to do was lie on the couch.

Deciding she'd had enough, Lauren tugged at Alex's shirt.

He cast a sideways glance and smiled but didn't slow his pace.

It appeared a more direct approach was indicated.

"Time for a break," Lauren announced. Instead of waiting for a response, she veered off the path, her eyes focused on an empty park bench under a tree.

Ignoring the peeling paint and possible splinters, Lauren collapsed onto the bench. In a second, Alex appeared beside her.

She wiped the perspiration from her face with the back of her hand and his gaze turned thoughtful.

"I'm sorry to make you stop," she said. "You can go on without me if you want to."

Alex smiled. "Actually I was ready for a break myself."

Lauren met his gaze. "I guess great minds think alike."

He slipped an arm around her shoulders. "Then you must know exactly what I'd like to do right now."

Though Lauren had never been big on public displays of affection, she might have let him kiss her…if not for the family of four headed their way. "You'd like to tell me about your childhood?"

Alex stared for a moment, nonplussed, then threw back his head and laughed. "You're right. That's just what I'd like to do."

Lauren laughed along with him and watched the family cycle past, feeling an unexpected pang of envy. Her parents had always been too busy to go on bike rides. Between her father's business ventures and her mother's social functions, there had been little time for anything else.

"Was your mother a full-time homemaker?"

The wistful quality in her voice surprised Alex and he smiled, thinking of his mother in such a role. Queen Genevieve had ruled Carpegnia since she'd been twenty-five. Her father had bypassed her two older brothers and picked her as his successor to the throne. Would Alex be bypassed in the same manner?

"Alex?"

He glanced up and realized Lauren expected an answer. "She's always worked full-time."

Alex thought about coming clean like he had with Sal and telling her the whole truth, but he wanted the time and setting to be just right. Sal's warning flashed before him, but he shoved it aside. He'd tell her *soon,* he promised himself, just not now. "She heads a large corporation."

"Sounds very demanding," Lauren said. "Does she travel a lot?"

"Not too much," Alex said. "But she often put in long hours. But my father was always around, so that helped."

Surprise skittered across Lauren's face as if she couldn't imagine a man making time for his children. "What does he do for a living?"

"He's a gardener."

"Really?" Instead of being put off at the thought of his father working with his hands, Lauren seemed intrigued.

Alex nodded. It wasn't entirely accurate, but when his father was asked about his occupation, that's what he said. His dad was modest to a fault and most people were amazed when they learned the queen's husband was actually considered to be one of the world's top designers of specialty gardens.

"Sounds like my kind of guy," Lauren said. "There's nothing I like more than planting seeds and watching them grow."

He smiled, remembering how she'd once said almost the same thing about her students.

"Have I told you lately how much I like being with you?" he asked suddenly.

A mischievous spark lit her eyes. "Does that mean we can walk the rest of the way?"

"Princess," he said. "We can do whatever you want."

Lauren laughed and her eyes sparkled like the finest emeralds. She looked so pretty sitting there in the sunlight that Alex couldn't resist. He leaned over and kissed her. Her lips were warm and tasted as sweet as the berries from his father's garden. Then one taste hadn't been enough. Now one kiss wasn't enough.

Her lips parted and he claimed her mouth, drinking her in. He pulled her closer, his fingers lost in the thick swirl of her hair. Her slender body felt firm and tight against him. He heard himself groan, a low sound of want and need that astonished him with its intensity. Dazed and breathing hard, he didn't try to stop her when she pulled back.

"I think we'd better start walking." Lauren brushed back a strand of hair from her face with a shaky hand and rose to her feet.

Alex stood and reached for her, but she took a step back. "I want to walk."

"No, you don't," Alex said, his gaze lingering on her lips. "You want to kiss me."

To his surprise, she laughed and shot him a teasing smile. "That may be so. But we're going to walk. And you're going to behave."

Alex heaved a resigned sigh and consoled himself with the knowledge they lived under the same roof. There would be plenty of other opportunities to kiss.

They strolled down the path for several minutes in silence.

"You said once your father was American." Lauren cast him a sideways glance. "I'm curious why your parents chose to make their home in Carpegnia rather than in the States?"

"My mother's job was there," Alex said with a shrug. "Living elsewhere wasn't an option."

Her brows drew together in thought.

"That must have been hard on your father," Lauren said finally. "Being so far from home."

"Carpegnia is a beautiful place." Alex found himself strangely disturbed by the comment. "My father considers it his home now."

"I'm not saying it isn't wonderful," Lauren said quickly.

"I'd like to show it to you some day," Alex said impulsively, knowing if she saw it she'd love it as he did. And for whatever reason, that suddenly seemed important. "Promise me you'll visit."

"It'll be at the top of my to-do list," Lauren said airily, shooting him an impish smile. "After I win the lottery, of course."

Irritation surged through Alex at the cavalier response. Didn't she understand how much he was going to miss her?

And worse yet, didn't she even care?

Chapter Eleven

"There's something different about you." Rusty leaned back in the kitchen chair and stared at Lauren, his gaze sharp and assessing.

She smiled and took a sip of lemonade. Trust Rusty to pick up on the smallest detail. Lauren pulled at a strand of hair. "I had a few highlights added last week."

Rusty shook his head. "I'm not talking about your hair. You just have this sort of glow about you."

"Glow?" Lauren laughed. "Yeah, right."

"You do," Rusty insisted. His gaze narrowed. "Is it because of him? Are you two serious?"

Lauren knew she could pretend she didn't understand whom Rusty was referring to, but that would be pointless. In the last couple of weeks, she and Alex had been inseparable. Every morning before work they ran for a half hour and every evening they had dinner together. On Sunday they attended church and last week they'd gone out with five or six couples for brunch.

Serious?

Rusty had been out of town, but from the speculative gleam in his eyes and his pointed questions, Lauren knew he'd caught up on all the latest gossip.

"Alex is only here for a few more months." Just saying the words brought a pang to her heart. "Then he'll be gone."

"Maybe he'll ask you to go with him."

Though that thought had crossed her mind several times, Lauren knew it wasn't going to happen. Alex had never given her any indication that their relationship would continue after he left.

"I don't think so."

Rusty knew her too well to be fooled by a cool manner and a few offhand words. "You love him."

The words slammed against her carefully constructed facade and for a moment Lauren thought she might crumble. But she took another sip of lemonade and steadied her composure before she spoke. She'd felt like a fool when David Warner had dumped her so publicly and she wasn't about to let that happen again.

"I like Alex," Lauren said, falling into her well-practiced way of skirting the truth. "But love him? I barely know him."

Alex stood in the hallway, just outside of the kitchen. He'd been disappointed when he pulled up and saw Rusty's car in the drive. Lauren had the day off school and Alex had slipped away from work early hoping to convince her to run errands with him.

He followed the sound of voices but before he could announce his presence, Alex heard his name.

"I like Alex," Lauren said. "But love him? I barely know him."

Though she wasn't saying anything he hadn't said to others who'd asked about their relationship, her casual dismissal stung. Surely she didn't believe they barely *knew* each other.

They'd spent a lot of time together the past couple of months and he'd enjoyed every minute. They even had a daily routine. He set the table while she prepared dinner. After they ate, he cleared the table. Since the dishwasher was still out of commission, they talked about their day while he washed and she dried. Afterward they'd walk down the quiet residential sidewalk holding hands. It sounded boring and mundane. But it wasn't, because he was with Lauren.

I barely know him. Alex's lips tightened.

He turned the corner and walked into the kitchen. Rusty and Lauren sat at the table, a coffee cake with two slices missing on the table between them.

The scent of cinnamon streusel filled the air and Alex's gaze lingered on the cake. "Something smells good."

Lauren looked up in surprise, her warm smile of welcome stilling his irritation. "You're early."

Somewhat mollified, he smiled. "I came home to change and see if you wanted to run errands with me."

Alex shifted his gaze to Rusty, who'd shoved back his chair and now stood shifting awkwardly from one foot to another. "Hello, Rusty."

"Alex." Rusty nodded pleasantly before turning his attention back to Lauren. "I hate to run but Aimee and I are headed to the lake and I promised I'd pick up a bucket of chicken."

"Aimee?" Alex tilted his head. "Carly's friend?"

"We've been seeing each other." Rusty flushed and the tips of his ears turned bright. "Carly still asks about you. I know she's interested, so if you—"

"I'm not," Alex said firmly, remembering what Lauren had said about giving a woman false hope. "Anyway, I already have a girlfriend."

Alex let his gaze linger on Lauren so there would be no misunderstanding. It only took a couple of seconds for her cheeks to turn as red as Rusty's ears.

Rusty's gaze shifted from Alex to Lauren and a knowing look filled his eyes. "So that's how it is."

"That's how it is," Alex said.

Less than five minutes later, Rusty was gone and Lauren was right where Alex wanted her—in his arms.

She toyed with the top button of his shirt. "So, you have a girlfriend, do you?"

The light scent of her perfume enveloped him, stirring his senses. Her fingers were like fire against his skin and he tightened his hold around her. "Yes, I do."

"Is she someone I know?" Lauren slipped the top button free.

"Intimately." He liked the feel of the word against his tongue, but he liked the feel of her soft body against his chest even more. He scattered kisses along her jawline.

"It's the middle of the day," she protested weakly even as she tilted her head back, giving him access to the creamy expanse of her neck.

"I can't think of anywhere I'd rather be." Alex smiled.

The sound she made was somewhere between a moan and a giggle. "In the kitchen?"

"No." He gently brushed her hair back from her face and lowered his mouth to hers. "With you."

Walking hand in hand with Alex through the crowded discount store was nice but Lauren couldn't help wishing she were back in the kitchen and in Alex's arms. This time, however, the scenario wouldn't include an unexpected phone call just when things were heating up.

The way things had been going, if her mother's call had come a few minutes later, she and Alex might have been in bed.

Just the thought set butterflies loose in Lauren's stomach. Over the past couple of months, she'd spent a great deal of time and put a lot of effort into not thinking about that night in the hotel room, which meant that it was practically all she thought about. Making Love had advanced to capitalized status in her mind.

And with each touch and kiss, she found herself longing to Make Love again and see if it really had been as fabulous as she remembered.

Today she'd been feeling particularly reckless. So what if he wasn't staying forever? He cared about her. She could see it in his face and in the thousand little things he did every day to make her life easier.

When Rusty had mentioned Carly, she'd wanted to slug him. What was he thinking? Trying to push another woman on the man she loved? Lauren caught her breath. Love? It was true. She didn't just *like* Alex, she *loved* him. Was it too much to hope that maybe, just maybe, he loved her too?

"Lauren." A familiar feminine voice broke

through her reverie and Lauren shifted her gaze in the direction of the voice. She smiled at the sight of Christy Warner with a baby in her arms and a toddler at her side. It was ironic, Lauren thought, that she should see her ex-boyfriend's wife when she was thinking about happily-ever-after. At one time Lauren had been convinced that she was going to marry David, Christy's husband of almost four years.

"Christy." Lauren handed Alex the items in her hand and enveloped the woman in a hug. "It's been way too long. And you, little man, I swear you've grown an inch since I last saw you." Lauren leaned over and tousled the boy's hair.

"It hasn't been *that* long," Christy said with a smile. But even before she finished speaking, the blonde's curious gaze had slid to Alex. "You're Tom Alvarez's friend, aren't you?"

Alex stepped forward, trying to place the woman but coming up blank. Nonetheless, he politely extended his hand. "Alex Gabrielle. Have we met?"

"No," Christy said. "But I feel like I know you already. I'm Christy Warner and Tom is my—"

"Publicist." Alex had immediately recognized the name. Christy was not only one of Tom's friends, but one of his biggest accounts—a psychologist turned motivational speaker. She was also married to Lauren's former boyfriend.

The blonde was beautiful and she seemed pleasant enough, but he couldn't imagine any man preferring her over Lauren.

Alex's lips twisted in a wry grin. Now he was beginning to think like Rusty.

"Are you two out…?"

"Running errands," Lauren said, including Alex in her smile. "School is out this week and Alex got home early."

"That's right." Christy juggled the baby who'd started to fuss. "Sara told me you two were living together."

"We live in the same house," Lauren clarified. Although Christy wasn't the type to gossip, Lauren did have an image to uphold, even among her friends. "Not really 'together,' if you know what I mean."

"Of course," Christy said quickly. Her cheeks turned a dusky pink. "I certainly didn't mean to imply—"

"You didn't." Lauren squeezed the woman's arm reassuringly. "I just don't want there to be any misunderstanding. You know how things are with the school. They practically expect us to be nuns."

Christy laughed. "I don't know how you stand the place."

"I love the children," Lauren said. "Speaking of children, hand me this little guy."

"He weighs a ton," Christy said, even as she handed the baby to Lauren.

"Sam is fat," Max exclaimed with all the tact of a four-year-old.

"Your brother is not fat," Christy gently scolded. "He's just a big boy."

"Fat," Max repeated.

This time Christy ignored him.

The baby fit perfectly in her arms and Lauren smiled. "You're right. He is heavy. How much does he weigh?"

Alex glanced in the direction of the check-out lines. Customers were backed up five deep. "I'm going to go ahead and pay. That'll give you two a chance to talk."

"Let me give you some money." Lauren reached for her purse but Alex shook his head.

"I'll cover you," he said, shooting her a wink. He said goodbye to Christy and headed for the shortest line.

Five minutes later, Alex was still waiting and the two women were still talking. The baby lay sound asleep against Lauren's chest, looking like he belonged there.

For one second, Alex let himself imagine that the baby was his. What would it be like to have a son or a daughter? And to see Lauren holding that child close? He smiled ruefully and shoved the image aside. It would be years before he was ready for the family-and-kids lifestyle. He had a kingdom to rule.

"That your wife?"

A raspy voice sounded behind Alex and he turned. A wiry gray-haired gentleman holding a bag of potting soil gestured with his head toward Lauren.

For a moment Alex wondered how the guy knew he and Lauren were even connected. Until he realized he hadn't taken his eyes off her since he'd gotten into line.

"No," Alex said. "I'm not married."

"Sure is pretty." The man stroked his whisker-stubbled chin. "How long you been married?"

It was obvious the guy was hard of hearing. Alex raised his voice. "She's not my wife."

"That your baby?"

Alex gritted his teeth. Was there something about shopping with a woman that branded you a family man? Or was the old man simply senile?

"If it were my baby—" Alex spoke slowly and distinctly so there would be no misunderstanding "—she'd be my wife."

"Pity," the man replied. "She's a pretty one."

"Yes, she is," Alex agreed. Lauren was also fun to be with and a good person deep inside where it really counted.

If he were looking to settle down, she'd certainly be the type of woman he'd want. Just thinking about leaving her made his heart ache. But the timing wasn't right.

Alex couldn't think about hearts and flowers or happily-ever-after when his whole future was at stake. He had to focus on the crown, on the one thing he'd wanted since he was a boy. And he couldn't let anyone, or anything, get in his way.

Chapter Twelve

"What do you mean you fainted at work?" Alex dropped his dessert fork to the table and his voice rose. "Why didn't you call me?"

"It was nothing."

"You blacked out but it was nothing?" His voice grew louder with each word and Lauren wished she'd kept her mouth shut.

"I think it was because I skipped breakfast and lunch," Lauren said. "And they've been working on the air-conditioning system at school, so the classroom was unbelievably hot."

"What did the doctor say?"

"I didn't see a doctor."

"You didn't—"

"The school nurse checked me out," she added hurriedly when his frown deepened.

"Sounds adequate to me." The sarcasm in his tone was tempered by the concern in his eyes.

"I made an appointment with the doctor for tomorrow." She shot him what she hoped was a reassuring smile. Personally, Lauren thought it was totally unnecessary but her principal had insisted.

"I'll take you," Alex said. "I have a couple of meetings but I'll cancel them."

"There's no need for you to do that," Lauren said hurriedly. "I feel perfectly fine."

"People who are perfectly fine don't faint."

"It's happened to me in the past," Lauren said. "It's no big deal."

Actually it had only happened once and that had been when she'd been six and was at the hospital getting stitches. Lauren saw no need to mention that fact.

"You're not doing a thing tonight," Alex said, "except sitting on the sofa and relaxing. Understand?"

By the look on Alex's face, Lauren knew it would be pointless to argue. "Okay, once the dishes are done, it's couch-potato time."

She shot him a cheeky grin but he didn't even crack a smile.

"You can sit at the table and supervise," he said. "But you're not helping."

"Kind of bossy, aren't you?"

"What I am is irritated you didn't call me when it happened," he said. "I worry about you."

Despite his brusque tone, the words filled her with warmth. "I'm fine."

"In fact, you're going to put your feet up right now."

Though Lauren normally hated taking orders, she was through with dessert and there was no reason not to do as he asked. Taking the hand he offered, Lauren let him lead her to the sofa and she lifted her legs obediently when he pushed the hassock close.

Another woman might have protested, but the concern in his eyes tugged at her heartstrings. She couldn't remember a time she'd felt so...loved.

Impulsively, Lauren patted the space beside her. "Sit with me for a few minutes."

To her surprise he didn't argue and when his arm slid around her shoulders, Lauren heaved a contented sigh.

"I want you to know," Alex said, "that I'll never let anyone or anything hurt you."

Lauren leaned back against his arm and gazed up at him, taking note of the strong jaw with a hint of stubbornness and the determined look in his eyes. Though he'd made her a promise he couldn't possibly keep, she still appreciated the sentiment.

All her life she'd had to be the strong one. She'd never had anyone she could lean on...until now.

She snuggled up to Alex and decided if she ever did marry it was definitely going to be to someone strong enough to lean on. Someone who cared enough to be her protector. And, if that someone also happened to be handsome and a great kisser, all the better.

Lauren stared at the doctor, a family practitioner who'd tended to her cuts and scrapes since she'd been a child. The room was deathly still, but her heart was pounding so hard, she was sure she'd misunderstood. "I'm pregnant?"

Dr. Taylor's expression softened at the distress in her voice. He nodded.

Lauren exhaled a ragged breath. It was obviously going to take more than a Band-Aid and some antiseptic to make this all better.

Tears sprang to her eyes but Lauren blinked them back and focused her gaze on the certificates hanging directly behind the doctor's desk. She struggled to regain her composure. "How far along am I?"

"Judging from the exam and the information you gave us, I'd say about nine weeks."

Chicago.

When she'd gone to the doctor about the fainting episode, Lauren had known in the back of her mind there was a *slight* chance she could be pregnant. But she'd decided early on that it was only a *very* slight possibility. After all, she'd known couples who'd tried for years to get pregnant without success. She'd decided that more than likely the light-headedness and missed cycles were due to the turmoil in her life.

Her kindergartners were a rambunctious group, her money was in short supply and her mother was still driving her crazy with her matchmaking schemes. Not to mention she had a handsome hunk of a man under the same roof who'd continued to make it clear with every kiss that he'd like a place in her bed. Who wouldn't be stressed?

"I take it this isn't happy news?" The doctor's gentle, fatherly tone was almost her undoing.

Lauren loved children and she wanted to be a mother. But some day. Not when she wasn't married. Not when she could barely make ends meet. Not when the man she loved was leaving in a couple of months.

"No," she said finally, clasping her hands in her lap to still their trembling. "It's definitely not happy news."

The doctor moved from behind the desk and crouched down beside her, taking her hand. "Sometimes the timing doesn't seem right."

For a second, Lauren thought he was just being sympathetic, telling her it was okay not to be excited.

"There are options." The doctor gave her a grave look. "Although I don't necessarily recommend taking any of those steps without counseling."

She realized what he was talking about and her hand moved protectively to her still-flat abdomen. "I couldn't do that."

"What about the father?" Dr. Taylor asked. "Will he support your decision?"

"He wouldn't want me to have an abortion, if that's what you're asking," Lauren said. Though they'd never discussed the controversial issue, she remembered his comments about his friend Harry doing the right thing. No, Alex wouldn't want her to have an abortion; he'd want her to marry him. In fact, he'd probably *insist* on getting married as soon as possible.

Although Lauren had always longed to be married and have a family, she wanted a marriage based on love, not on honor. And, although she knew she loved Alex, she still didn't know if he returned those feelings.

"The nurse will get some family history then give you a packet of information you and the father can review together. I also want to start you on some prenatal vitamins."

The doctor patted her hand. "We'll see you in four weeks. He can come with you to that appointment if he'd like."

Lauren smiled wanly. Four weeks from now, Alex would be putting the finishing touches on Sara's tour plans…and making plans to leave.

Unless I tell him about the baby. Then he'll stay. Or he'll ask me to go with him.

The possibility that once would have filled her with excitement now held a bittersweet edge. If she told him she was pregnant, they'd be together forever. His sense of honor wouldn't have it any other way.

But she wanted him to be with her because he *wanted* to, not because he *had* to.

That meant she had no choice.

This baby was going to have to be her little secret. At least until she discovered Alex's true feelings.

It had been a perfectly horrible day, Alex decided. It had started when Lauren had refused to let him take her to the doctor. Then the traffic on the interstate had been backed up and he'd missed his ten o'clock meeting. To make matters worse, at the last minute Sara had decided she needed more than one night's break between the concerts in France and Italy and he'd had to do some major reshuffling.

Still, Alex could have weathered these crises if he'd been able to reach Lauren and find out the results of her appointment. He'd kept his cell phone close, but she hadn't called. And when he'd called her cell phone number, it went immediately to voice mail. The whole day had been extremely aggravating.

When he turned the corner and saw her car sitting

in the driveway, he breathed a sigh of relief. At least she'd made it home.

The minute Alex opened the door, a tantalizing aroma greeted him and he knew just where to find her. He sidestepped four large shopping bags sitting in the hall and headed straight for the kitchen.

She was at the stove, stirring a pot of bubbling marinara. He expected her to look up when he entered the room, but her gaze remained riveted to the stove as if the simmering sauce demanded her total attention.

"I tried to call your cell but I couldn't—"

"I forgot to turn it on," Lauren said, finally looking up.

The phone was her lifeline and he didn't for one moment believe she'd forgotten to turn it on, which meant she'd deliberately avoided his calls. His first reaction was pure annoyance. But his heart froze in his chest at the strain edging her eyes.

"How'd the doctor's visit go?"

Her lips curved dutifully upward but the smile didn't quite reach her eyes. "I'm healthy as a horse."

Alex eyed her suspiciously. "If you're so healthy, why did you faint?"

She waved a vague hand and her attention returned to the sauce.

"Something about not eating or low blood pressure," she mumbled. "Nothing of any real significance."

He closed the distance between them and turned her to face him. "Tell me the truth."

Her eyes softened at the concern in his voice. "I'm fine. Really."

"Tell me the truth," he repeated.

"I am," she insisted, fumbling with the stirring spoon, her cheeks flushed with color from the stove. "It's just my body telling me I've been trying to do too much. The doctor says I need to get more sleep and make sure I eat regularly."

Knowing Lauren as he did, the explanation made sense to Alex. She often stayed up late and hadn't she told him more than once how much she hated eating school lunches?

Alex heaved a relieved sigh and pulled her into his arms, feeling the tension that had twisted his stomach into a knot ease. He'd worried the problem had been serious. Now that he knew it was something easily manageable, he felt like celebrating. "Let's go out tonight."

"Can't," Lauren said with a wry smile. "I'm broke."

Alex thought about the sacks of clothes in the hall and decided broke was definitely an understatement.

"My treat." He offered her his most persuasive smile.

Her gaze lowered to the sauce.

"It'll keep."

She hesitated. "I don't know if—"

The phone's ring cut off her words.

"Ignore it," Alex said.

Lauren shook her head. "I can't. Sara and I are meeting tomorrow and it's probably her calling to firm things up."

She reached over and picked up the receiver. Immediately two tiny lines of worry appeared between her brows. "Yes, he's right here."

"Alex." She held the phone out to him. "It's your mother. She says it's imperative she speak with you."

The knot returned to Alex's stomach with a vengeance. He'd given his parents Lauren's home number for emergencies but he'd never expected them to use it.

He flashed Lauren a reassuring smile and took the phone, his palms suddenly damp with sweat. "Mother?"

"I'm sorry to call you."

The minute Alex heard the tremble in his mother's voice he knew whatever she'd called about was indeed serious.

Icy fingers of fear traveled up his spine.

"What is it?" he asked. "Has something happened to Dad?"

"Your father is fine," his mother said quickly. "He's standing right here beside me."

"Is it your dad?" Lauren whispered.

Alex shook his head, his attention focused on the phone. "Tell me what's going on."

"It's Luc," his mother said. "He's missing."

"Missing?" Alex's voice rose despite his best efforts to control it. "How can he be missing?"

He listened in horror as his mother recounted how she hadn't heard from his youngest brother in the last month but hadn't been worried...until the police had called. Luc's wallet had been found in New York City. The money and credit cards were gone.

Apparently there had been an accident at that corner earlier in the day and the police had discovered the wallet during their investigation.

"What do the police think?" Alex asked.

"They don't know." His mother's voice broke then steadied. "But they're concerned."

"Do they think he's been kidnapped?" Carpegnia was a small country but a wealthy one.

"They don't know," his mother repeated. "We have to wait and see if we get a ransom demand."

She didn't say what would happen if they didn't get a ransom note or call, and Alex didn't ask. He didn't want to even think about that possibility. Luc was a headstrong, opinionated young man whom Alex loved with an intensity that took his breath away. If anything happened to him...

Alex wiped a shaky hand across his forehead. "What can I do to help?"

"Gabe has commitments that make it difficult for him to leave at this time," his mother said. "We really need a family member in Boston to work with the police and the FBI."

"I'll be on the next plane out," Alex said.

"I was hoping you'd say that." Even across the ocean and half a continent, Alex could hear the relief in his mother's voice. "We've booked you a flight to Boston first thing tomorrow morning."

"Tomorrow?" Alex's fingers tightened around the receiver. Hadn't he read somewhere that the first twenty-four hours were the most critical? "What about tonight?"

"You wouldn't get in until late," his mother said. "You'll do more good if you get a good night's sleep."

"Sleep?" Alex fairly shouted the word into the phone. "How can I sleep when my brother is missing?"

Alex felt Lauren's hand on his arm and he turned to find her looking up at him, her face filled with worry. His arm slipped around her waist and he pulled her close, drawing strength from her nearness.

He listened while his mother relayed the flight information, instructing him to contact her once he landed in Boston.

"Call me if you hear anything," he ordered right before he hung up.

"What's the matter?" Lauren asked. "Is your brother all right?"

"We don't know." He quickly filled her in on the other end of the phone conversation.

"They think he may have been kidnapped?" Her voice came out as a tiny squeak.

"It's not common for royalty," Alex said. "But it does happen."

Lauren stilled. "Royalty?"

The look on her face sent unease coursing through Alex. This wasn't how he'd wanted to break it to her. But she'd read about it tomorrow in the press and he'd rather she heard it from him.

"My mother is the queen of Carpegnia," Alex said. "That makes my brother a prince."

"A prince?" Lauren asked with a dazed look.

"I know. This is a shock. I wish I had more time to explain—"

"That means you're a prince, too." Her expression could have been carved in stone.

"Don't be angry," Alex said. "Not now. Please. I need you to be here for me."

Don't be angry? Be there for me?

How dare he?

The man had lived under her roof, eaten her food and lied to her all these months and he thought she shouldn't be angry?

Lauren's hands clenched into fists at her sides even as her stomach lurched. She tried to calm her rioting emotions, knowing stress wasn't good for the baby.

Oh my God, the baby. My baby's father is a prince.

A nervous giggle rose in her throat at the thought of her mother's elation if she got wind of this. Snagging a prince would surpass Clarice's wildest expectations. Except her mother would never learn of this little detail. Because Alex was a liar, a player, a man who obviously didn't care enough to tell her his true identity.

She'd thought they'd become close these last few weeks. She'd thought he cared. But he'd merely been killing time, fooling around with the local girl until it was time to go back to his castle. But why had he pretended to be broke? She shoved the question aside. What did it matter? What did any of it matter?

Lauren took a shaky step backward, her mind racing even as deep, numbing fatigue filled her. *A prince.* She didn't know anything about royalty except that bloodlines were all-important.

Bloodlines.

What if he wants to take my baby?

Fear shot through her with a force that took her breath away. Dear God, no. Not my baby.

"Lauren," Alex's voice pulled her from her thoughts.

She stared at him and saw the naked misery on his

face. Lauren wanted to hate him, but she couldn't. Though Alex had rarely talked about Luc, she knew he loved his brother deeply. When he opened his arms, Lauren moved forward and let him pull her close.

Thinking she could remain rational and distant while she comforted him was her first mistake. The minute his arms closed around her, the tears began to fall.

Tears for her.

Tears for him.

But most of all, tears for a little baby who would never have the chance to know its father.

Chapter Thirteen

Four o'clock in the morning and Lauren hadn't slept a wink. All night her mind had raced, trying to figure out a future for herself...and a baby. A future that suddenly seemed barren and empty. A future without the man she loved.

A knock sounded on her bedroom door and before she could even respond, it eased open. She hadn't thought to lock it. There had been no need. Alex had always respected her privacy.

He moved quietly through the room and sat on the edge of the bed. He smelled of shampoo and soap and that spicy, somewhat exotic cologne that she associated with him alone. The scent was so familiar it brought tears to her already swollen eyes.

But when she finally found her voice, she sounded more cross than sad. "What are you doing in my room?"

"I came to say goodbye," he said softly. "I have to leave for the airport in a few minutes."

This was it, Lauren realized. The end. There would be no happily-ever-after for her. Once Alex walked out the door, it was over.

A great aching pain squeezed her heart, an overpowering wish that somehow things could have been different. If only he could have loved her even half as much as she loved him.

Lauren choked back a sob.

Unexpectedly Alex leaned over and lay his head against her belly, and it struck her that this was the closest he'd ever be to his child.

Dear God, could this be any harder?

"I should have told you who I was from the very beginning," he said in a tone so low she had to strain to hear.

"It doesn't matter." She resisted the urge to stroke his hair one last time.

"Yes, it does," Alex said. "I hurt you and I'm truly sorry. I don't want to leave with this between us."

Lauren blinked back her tears.

"This isn't goodbye." He raised himself to a sitting position and even in the semi-darkness she could see the determined gleam in his eyes. "Once Luc is found…"

His stopped for a heartbeat before clearing his throat and continuing. "I promise you we'll see each other again."

His voice was strong and confident and, even to her cynical ears, sincere. But maybe that was because she wanted so much to believe him. Still, the last thing she needed was to cling to false hope.

"Don't, Alex," she said, a trace of desperation in her tone. "Don't do this to me."

"Do what?" Surprise filled his voice.

"Don't make a promise you can't keep." Her voice grew stronger with each word. "Just say goodbye. Say it was good while it lasted. Say years from now you'll look back on the time you spent in St. Louis and think of me with fondness."

"Fondness?" he bellowed, his voice filling the small room and echoing off the walls. "Is that all you think you mean to me?"

Before she could answer, a honk sounded from the driveway, followed quickly by another one.

An expletive slipped past his lips.

Lauren pushed herself up to her elbows. "You'd better go."

Alex raked his fingers through his hair. "I don't want to leave like this."

When he made no move to get up, Lauren cast a

pointed glance at the clock. "If you don't leave now," she said. "You'll miss your flight."

The horn sounded again and before she'd even realized what was happening, Alex leaned over and brushed a kiss across her lips.

"This isn't goodbye," he said. "I *will* be back."

He rose from the bed and headed for the door.

It was her last chance to stop him. Regardless of what he said, she knew this was the last time they'd be together.

A weaker woman would have ignored the fact that he needed to help his brother. Would have broken down and begged him to stay. Would have used the baby to force him to stay. But Lauren had never been weak. She'd been through her share of hard times and she'd survived.

This would be no exception.

She lifted her hand in farewell. "Goodbye, Alex."

Day 1

Dear Lauren,
Tried to call but your cell phone must have been off. Landed safely. Met with the detective in charge of Luc's case and with a team from the FBI. Awaiting a ransom demand. I miss you.

Alex

Lauren stared at the e-mail. He'd called her "dear" and said he missed her. Though she didn't want to cling to false hope, maybe he *would* be back. After all, he didn't have to e-mail her. Or call. Did he?

Day 30

Dear Lauren,
Very little progress in the investigation. Police are puzzled. No ransom demands but thankfully no body. It's like Luc has dropped off the face of the earth. I know the police are losing hope but I am still firmly convinced my brother is alive.

It was great talking to you yesterday. Thanks for letting me explain. I hope you now understand why I didn't initially tell you about my background. It was never my intent to hurt you. I hope you can forgive me …

I was sorry to hear you'd moved. I know the town house was expensive, but I hoped you'd be able to afford to stay. I just wish you'd at least considered taking the money I offered. That said, I'm happy you were able to find a place that didn't require a lease. If it's not exactly what you want and you don't like it, you don't have to stay…
Alex

Lauren glanced around the two-bedroom bunga-
low. It was old and shabby and not at *all* what she
wanted. But the area was safe and the rent cheap.
Though it would be months before the baby arrived,
she'd had to face the fact that she couldn't save
money as long as she was paying such exorbitant
rent. And she refused to take money from Alex.

When her landlord had casually mentioned he
had someone interested in renting a unit, Lauren had
offered hers. Her friends hadn't understood why she
wanted to move, but then how could they? They
thought she was carefree and single. They didn't
know she was flat broke with a baby on the way.

Day 45

Dear Lauren,
Thanks for the e-mail but I have to say it's
not the same as talking to you.

I've been keeping busy handling the family's North American business while working with the private detectives we've hired to
help with the investigation. The Boston police
are doing their best but their resources are
limited and Luc's case is growing colder by the
day. We're all hoping the million-dollar re-
ward will bring in some new leads.

Sounds like your part-time job at Nordstrom and teaching are keeping you busy....

Alex

Busy? Lauren swallowed a hysterical laugh. Busy didn't begin to describe her life. Her friends thought she'd taken the sales position at Nordstrom for the employee discount. The truth was she was trying to get all her bills paid off before the baby came and it was turning out to be a monumental task.

She'd cut back to bare bones but it still wasn't enough. Every once in a while she'd treat herself to a scone and a cappuccino and daydream about a handsome prince unexpectedly showing up and proclaiming his love. But deep down Lauren knew those outcomes were reserved for the pages of storybooks or the movie screen, not for elementary-school teachers stuck in the real world.

Day 62

Dear Lauren,
Luc has been found! My mother is already planning a big welcome home celebration. Physically he's in good shape. Mentally he's still a little shaky. He doesn't remember anything that happened during the last couple of months but the doctors are hopeful that, with time, his memory will return.

I wish you were here to share my joy.
Alex

I wish you were here to share my joy.

When she'd seen Alex on TV, Lauren had cried. He'd looked so good, so happy with a big smile blanketing his face that she'd wanted so much to call and talk to him. She'd even been tempted to tell him about the baby. It had seemed like fate when the phone had rung and he'd been on the line.

But she'd never had the chance and Alex hadn't mentioned anything about returning to St. Louis. All he could talk about was Luc and how he couldn't wait to get his brother back home.

Day 65

Dear Lauren,
I think about you all the time and wonder how you're doing. Sounds like everything is going well for you. Luc and I head back to Carpegnia today.

I wished there would have been some time for a quick trip to St. Louis, but I couldn't fit it in. I hope you understand...
Alex

I couldn't fit it in....

Tears filled Lauren's eyes and she had a sudden urge to slam her hand through the computer screen. Instead she took a deep, steadying breath and scolded herself. Why was she getting so upset? Wasn't this just what she'd thought would happen? Hadn't she learned long ago that promises were just words?

But when Alex had gone out of his way to stay in touch, she'd hoped he would prove her wrong. Now, she had to decide what she was going to do. She couldn't have him stopping by in the future and discovering he had a child. Family was important to Alex, and Lauren had no doubt he'd do everything in his power to see that his child was raised in Carpegnia. And he'd have the money and resources to make that happen.

Though the thought of totally cutting him out of her life broke her heart, she didn't see where she had much choice. She had to protect her child.

Day 79

Lauren,
I was shocked to get your e-mail. Why would you ask me to stop communicating?

Was it something I said? Something I did?

I know these past weeks have been difficult for you, but they haven't been easy for me either.

We need to talk. I'll call you at eight o'clock.
Alex

Lauren glanced at the clock. Seven fifty-five. She

hadn't yet decided whether she was going to answer the phone when it rang because she wasn't sure what to say.

She'd finally accepted the fact that she'd merely been a momentary distraction, something that had been fun while it lasted, but a relationship never intended to go the distance. Her e-mail had made it clear that whatever they'd had was over and that she didn't want to see him again…ever. What was there to talk about?

Alex stared at the phone, his stomach a mass of knots. He felt as nervous as a schoolboy about to ask a girl for a first date.

When he'd read Lauren's last e-mail he'd been stunned. Didn't she realize these past months had been hard on him, too? Not only had be been worried about his brother, he'd missed her with an intensity that had taken him by surprise. It was like half of him was missing when she wasn't by his side.

That's why he'd made such an effort to keep in touch. A hundred times or more, he'd wanted to forget the investigation, hop on a plane and find solace in her arms. But he couldn't. He'd owed it to his brother and his family to stay the course. But with each missed call, each impersonal e-mail, he'd felt Lauren slipping away.

He'd promised himself that once his brother was

found, he'd return to St. Louis. But he hadn't counted on Luc's mental state. His brother hadn't been able to remember anything that had happened to him in the months since he'd vanished from that Boston street. Luc needed family beside him when he returned to Carpegnia. And now, with the Ceremony of the Sacred Sword quickly approaching, there was no time.

He'd hoped she'd understand. But from her last e-mail, it appeared she didn't. Not at all.

Picking up the phone, Alex punched in the numbers, cursing the fear edging his nerves and reminding himself if she couldn't comprehend a man's duty to family and country, she wasn't the woman he thought she was.

The phone conversation wasn't going as Lauren had planned. Alex was being surprisingly bullheaded about discontinuing all contact.

Lauren thought for a moment then forced a reasonable tone. "Why is it so hard for you to understand that I'm just not interested in keeping in touch?"

"I know it hasn't been easy being apart—"

"Actually, I haven't thought much about it. I've been so busy..." Lauren took a deep steadying breath and lied through her teeth. "The fact is, Alex, I've moved on."

"You have a new boyfriend?" Even across the

phone lines the shock in Alex's voice was palpable. "I thought you and I—"

"C'mon, Alex, get real." Though Lauren had the receiver in a death grip, her voice sounded surprisingly natural. "What we had was fun while it lasted but now it's over. You have your life. I have mine."

"I want to see you," Alex said, a determined thread underlying his words. "Things are settling down here. I can't come right now, but I should be able to get away soon."

Soon. It was such an ambiguous word. It could mean in a day, a week, a year.

Silence filled the phone line and Lauren found herself wondering what it would be like to be in the same room with Alex again. To look into his eyes, smell his cologne, feel his arms holding her tight...

"We can talk," Alex said eagerly as if sensing an opening. "Clear the air. I could—"

"No." The word shot out of her mouth like a bullet and Lauren realized that for a split second she'd allowed herself to hope for what she knew could never be.

"I don't want to see you again, Alex." She drew a ragged breath and steadied her resolve. "Not now. Not in a few weeks. Not ever."

It was the beginning of the end. Lauren pushed every button she could think of, said whatever she could to provoke him until his anger had flared. By

Chapter Fourteen

It must have been seeing Alex's face on the television that made her feel especially weepy, Lauren decided. She took a sip of her Italian soda and glanced at the clock on the bistro's wall.

According to the morning news report, the ceremony to announce who would be the next king of Carpegnia was set for later in the week. Dignitaries from all of Europe were expected to attend and speculation was that Alex would be the one to get the nod.

It had been well over a month since they'd talked. She still missed Alex but she'd done what she had to do to protect herself and the baby.

Lauren's hand dropped to rest on her growing

belly. Each day her pregnancy became harder to hide. She'd avoided her friends and told the ones she did see that she was into loose and comfortable clothing this summer. So far it had worked, but it wouldn't for much longer.

Lauren was going to have to tell them she was pregnant…and soon. She'd decided to say the father was someone she'd met in Chicago, someone she hadn't seen since, someone she didn't expect to see again.

Although she and Alex had danced together at the reception, they'd left at different times so there was no way anyone would suspect him. And their last conversation guaranteed he wouldn't be coming around.

Her heart ached remembering the angry, hurtful words they'd exchanged over the phone. But even as she was inciting him, she'd known it was for the best. She'd had to make it clear that there was nothing for him in St. Louis. That was the only way she could be sure he wouldn't just up and stop by when it was convenient.

"I'm sorry I'm late." Clarice Carlyle, looking quite summery in her yellow linen suit, pulled out a chair and took a seat opposite Lauren. "Traffic was horrid. I hope I didn't keep you waiting long."

Lauren offered a noncommittal smile. Actually, she'd found herself hoping her mother wouldn't show at all. That way she could postpone telling her about the baby, which was the reason for the impromptu luncheon. Though Lauren really wasn't up on the proper etiquette related to out-of-wedlock pregnancy announcements, it seemed to her that parents should be told first.

"I did get a little hungry," Lauren admitted. "But the waiter brought me a selection of appetizers to munch on while I waited."

Clarice's gaze shifted from Lauren to the half-eaten platter of food, then back to her daughter. A look of disapproval crossed her face. "Lauren, honey, you need to remember you're not as young as you once were and if you're not careful you're going to end up just like Marlene. Then you can kiss your chances of finding a man goodbye."

Marlene was Clarice's sister, a lovely woman who'd struggled with her weight for as long as Lauren could remember. From her mother's pointed comments, Lauren concluded that her baggy clothes hadn't concealed her expanding girth quite as well as she'd hoped.

"I'm not interested in finding a man," Lauren said. It was a calculated move. She knew full well making that comment to her mother was akin to waving a red flag at a bull. But if her mother responded true to form, it would be the perfect lead-in to her announcement.

"Not interested?" Clarice frowned. "What are you talking about? Of course, you're interested. You're only thirty. You're in the prime of life. You're—"

"I'm pregnant."

Clarice gasped and sat back in her chair, one hand rising to her throat. Her carefully made-up face was suddenly as white as the pristine tablecloth.

As tempted as Lauren was to fill the ensuing silence, she forced herself to sit quietly and give her mother time to absorb the news.

"Are you sure?" Clarice said at last.

Lauren nodded. "I'm in my sixth month."

"And you're just now telling me?" Clarice's eyes blazed. "Who else knows?"

"No one," Lauren said. "You're the first person I've told."

"What about the father?"

Lauren shook her head. "He's not in the picture."

Her mother's gaze narrowed. "Who is he?"

"You don't know him." Though she'd practiced the response in her head while waiting, Lauren's lips stumbled over the words.

"You never were a good liar." Her mother paused for a long moment, and then her lips curved upward. "It's Alex Gabrielle, isn't it?"

"Alex?" Lauren widened her gaze.

Clarice's smile widened in satisfaction. "I must say I like the idea of having a prince for a son-in-law."

"Sorry. Not him." Lauren somehow managed a slight smile and a flip tone. "Alex is a good-looking guy and I can't say I wasn't tempted but we never slept together while he was under my roof."

At least that part was true, and even to Lauren's critical ear, it sounded sincere.

Her mother's smile disappeared. "Then who?"

"I told you," Lauren repeated. "No one you know."

"I don't believe you." A look of sudden horror crossed Clarice's face. "Don't tell me it's that red-headed friend of yours?"

"Aaron?" Her mother had never liked Rusty and for a second Lauren was tempted to say it *was* him just to get her mother off her back. But common sense won out and she shook her head. "Rusty and I are just friends. The father is a man I met when I was in Chicago for Melanie's wedding. It was just a one-night thing."

"Is he rich?" A gleam replaced the distress in Clarice's eyes. "Even if he's married, that can be worked around."

"You know I would never sleep with a married man," Lauren snapped.

"That's right." A calculating look filled her mother's gaze. "I remember now. You made a special point to tell me he was single."

"When did I tell you that?" Lauren searched her

memory, trying desperately to recall such a conversation.

"Right after you'd gotten back from the wedding," Clarice said. "You mentioned you'd met someone at the reception. An old friend of Tom Alvarez. An out-of-work friend."

Her mother wrinkled her nose.

A cold shiver went through Lauren. How could she have forgotten? This put a chink in her lie. If her mother mentioned this information to anyone who happened to be at the wedding, it would be easy for them to figure out that the man she'd been talking about was Alex.

"Sara mentioned that she'd interviewed Alex while she was in Chicago for that wedding," her mother continued when Lauren didn't speak. "He's a friend of Tom Alvarez. And he was unemployed. Of course, that scarcely matters now."

"It mattered to you at the time," Lauren retorted. "You said he wasn't good enough for me."

Clarice laughed as if Lauren had said something extremely amusing. "That was before I knew he was a prince. And worth billions."

"It's always about money with you, isn't it?" Disappointment washed over Lauren and she couldn't quite keep the bitterness from her tone.

"Sweetheart, that's not fair." Clarice leaned across the table and patted Lauren's hand as if she were three and not thirty. "Your father and I only want what's best for you. That's all we've ever wanted."

"The best for me is not a man who doesn't love me." The feelings Lauren had kept pent up inside suddenly surged forward, demanding release. "I don't care how much money the man has or doesn't have, I want someone who is with me because he loves me. I don't want anyone with me out of obligation. Do you understand?"

Clarice nodded but Lauren wasn't convinced.

"So even if you knew who my baby's father was, you wouldn't say anything, not to anyone," Lauren continued, driving the point home. "Right?"

A hurt look skittered across Clarice's face. "What kind of question is that? I would never do something so underhanded. Have a little faith in your mother."

Lauren leaned forward, her gaze sharp and assessing. "Not one word. Not to anyone."

"All right," Clarice said, clearly disgusted. "But I think you're being extremely foolish."

"Foolish or not, it's what I want." Impulsively, Lauren reached across the table and gave her mother's hand a quick squeeze. "I'm glad I can count on your support."

The sidewalk café in the little village was deserted. It was too late for lunch and too early for dinner. But for Alex and his brother Luc, the solitude was a welcome change from all the activity at the castle.

Preparations were in high gear for Friday's ceremony, but ever since Lauren had told him she never wanted to see him again, Alex hadn't been able to summon up much enthusiasm.

"So, who is she?" Luc asked.

Alex took a sip of his beer and glanced across the table. "What do you mean?"

"Ever since we returned from the States, you haven't been yourself," Luc said. "You can't be worried about Friday since everyone knows you're going to be the next—"

"Luc," Alex interrupted. "That's media hype. Pure speculation."

Alex knew his mother had been impressed with his ability to live within his means and the way he'd handled things in Boston. Still, there were no guarantees in life. And even if he didn't receive the Sacred Sword, the world would go on. These past couple of months had taught Alex there were more important things than ruling a country.

"Whatever you say, Your Highness." Luc lowered his head in an exaggerated bow, and then laughed. "Anyway, tell me about this woman. Who is she? Do I know her?"

Alex smiled. Though he wasn't sure how he felt about interrogation, it was good to see the spark back in his brother's eye. "She's a schoolteacher. We shared a house in St. Louis."

And I miss her terribly, Alex added silently to himself.

His gaze drifted down the cobblestone street, taking in the quaint little shops lining both sides of the narrow road. He could picture Lauren coming in and out of the stores, her arms laden with sacks, her face flushed with excitement. An ache filled his heart.

"What's her name?"

Alex sighed and shifted his gaze back to his brother.

"It doesn't matter," Alex said. "She blew me off. Told me she never wanted to see me again."

Instead of laughing and teasing his brother about losing his touch, Luc leaned back in his chair and steepled his fingers beneath his chin. "Why'd she do that?"

It was the same question Alex had been asking himself. When he'd finally cooled down after their last conversation and had been able to think rationally, he'd realized Lauren had deliberately picked a fight with him. The question was—why?

"The only thing I can figure is that she thought I didn't care," Alex said. "And she wanted to dump me before I dumped her."

Given her past experience with David Warner, it made sense.

"Did you?" Luc cast Alex a speculative look. "Care, I mean?"

"I didn't promise her anything," Alex said almost to himself. "Because I knew I'd be leaving at the end of the summer."

Luc took another sip of beer. "So it was just about sex?"

"It wasn't about sex." Alex slammed his mug against the table. He couldn't deny he'd enjoyed kissing Lauren and the memory of the night they'd spent together still made his blood burn, but what they'd shared had been so much more than physical.

"I loved her," he said fiercely. "I still love her."

The words hung in the air. It shouldn't have seemed so profound, but there was something about saying it out loud, about admitting it to Luc and to himself that made it real.

No wonder his life had seemed flat and empty since leaving St. Louis and the thought of being crowned king at the end of the week hadn't filled him with excitement. Because something was missing. Some *one* was missing. Without Lauren, he was incomplete.

"If you love her," Luc said with an intense gaze, "why isn't she here with you?"

"I never thought to ask her. When I got the call about you, I had to leave immediately and then things just snowballed from there." Alex raked his fingers through his hair and blew out a frustrated breath. Looking back, he wished he had sent for her as soon as Luc had been found. "I really screwed up."

"Then go to her. Grovel. Tell her that you're lower than an earthworm," Luc suggested. "Women love that kind of thing."

Though Alex had never groveled, he wasn't above doing it if it meant Lauren would be back in his arms. "It may be too late."

"It's never too late," Luc said, waving a dismissive hand. "What a prince wants, a prince gets."

Luc's arrogant decree brought the smile back to Alex's face. When they were growing up, the three brothers had been firmly convinced the world was theirs for the taking.

Alex hoped that belief would be upheld. Because this time it wouldn't be just his pride that would be on the line.

It would be his heart.

Lauren answered the door on the first ring. Her gaze settled on Alex and the smile immediately faded. "What are you doing here?"

She looked so good in sweats and an oversized Cardinals T-shirt that he had to resist the urge to pull her to him, to breathe in the scent of her, to once again feel the softness of her hair against his cheek. Instead he rocked back on his heels and met her gaze. "May I come in?"

She kept her hand on the doorknob. "I don't think that's a good idea."

"I've flown all this way to see you," he said. "Surely you can spare a few minutes."

Her eyes glittered like emeralds in a face that suddenly seemed way too pale. "My mother called, didn't she?"

Alex frowned. There had been a message to call Clarice right before he'd left Carpegnia. He'd tried but hadn't been able to reach her.

"I haven't talked to your mother since I left St. Louis," he said. "Should I have?"

Though Lauren's expression didn't waver, Alex got the feeling she didn't believe him. "You need to go."

"I'm not leaving until we talk."

"So, talk."

Alex couldn't believe it. The concrete stoop was barely big enough for two people and not at all suitable for what he had to say. But he didn't have much choice.

"Why are you here, Alex?" Lauren asked when he didn't speak. "I thought I'd made it clear I didn't want to see you again."

"I've come to ask you to marry me." Alex pulled the ring from his pocket and bent down on one knee. "Lauren, please do me the honor of saying you'll be my wife."

Chapter Fifteen

A myriad of emotions skittered across Lauren's face and for a second Alex caught a glimpse of the Lauren he knew and loved before the polite mask descended.

"I'm afraid I have to decline," she said. "Thanks anyway."

"Thanks anyway?" Alex rose to his feet and his fingers closed around the ring. "I asked you to *marry* me."

Lauren lifted her chin. "And I said no."

"That's crazy."

"Why? Because I'm not falling all over myself in gratitude that the future king of Carpegnia wants to do right by me?"

The bitterness in her tone surprised him almost as much as her words. "What are you talking about?"

"My mother got to you, didn't she?" Lauren's lips pressed together. "Obviously her promise meant nothing."

Alex didn't know what issue she had with her mother, but whatever the problem was, he wished Lauren could just set it aside for a few minutes and focus on them.

"I don't want to talk about your mother," Alex said. "I want to talk about us. I'm here because I love you. Because I want to marry you."

"Stop with the lies." Her eyes blazed and her hands fisted at her sides. "You're only here because of the baby and we both know it."

"Baby?" Alex could only stare as the world around him spun. He searched his memory. It couldn't be. That long-ago morning in the hotel room, Lauren had insisted it was the wrong time of the month and that there was no way she could get pregnant. She'd been so sure that he'd taken her at her word and hadn't given the matter another thought.

But now, thinking back he remembered the fatigue, the nausea and her fainting spell.

He took a deep steadying breath and focused his gaze on her midsection. If he hadn't been looking carefully, he might not have noticed. The oversized

St. Louis Cardinals T-shirt she was wearing hid a lot. But he *was* looking and he *did* notice.

He clenched his jaw. How could she have kept such a secret from him? By God, he was the father. He deserved to know.

Alex met her gaze. "When were you going to tell me?"

She lifted her chin defiantly and remained silent.

A shock of realization shot through him. "You weren't going to tell me, were you? This was going to be your little secret."

"This is *my* baby," she said. "None of this has anything to do with you."

"You're wrong," Alex said, a steely edge to his voice. "It has everything to do with me."

"I'd like you to leave."

Her eyes flashed but the tremble in her voice stopped his sharp retort and he suddenly realized what he'd done. He'd left her to deal with this alone.

All her life she'd been on her own. Her parents had been too busy doing their own thing. He hadn't been much better. Not telling him was inexcusable. But what he'd done was equally inexcusable.

"I'm not going anywhere," he said. "Not until you agree to marry me."

"It's okay, Alex," she said, her voice growing stronger with each word. "I'm not like your friend Harry's girlfriend. I know my mother would die if she heard me say this, but I don't want a man who is with me because he feels obligated, no matter how rich he is."

"Obligated?"

"Yes, obligated," Lauren repeated. "With me because of a sense of honor."

Alex frowned. "I love you."

"You came because my mother called and told you I was pregnant."

"How many times do I have to tell you?" Alex's voice rose in frustration. "I haven't talked to Clarice since I left St. Louis and I had no idea you were pregnant until you told me."

Lauren paused. His surprise had seemed genuine and the look in his eyes appeared sincere. Not to mention her mother *had* promised to keep her mouth shut....

"And for your information I don't want to be with you for any other reason than because I love you," Alex continued.

"If you loved me, you'd have been here a long time ago."

"I had to stay in Boston."

"I'm not talking about Boston," Lauren said. "I'm talking about the past month. Since your brother was found."

"You're right," he said. "I should have come once I'd gotten everything settled. But you told me you never wanted to see me again, that I'd been just a momentary diversion and you were tired of me."

Two bright spots of color appeared on each cheek but she remained silent.

"Still I shouldn't have listened. I should have made it clear then that you were the most important thing in my life." Alex put his hands on her arms and stared straight into her eyes. "I've been blind and stupid and I deserve to have you hate me forever. I'm lower than an earthworm."

Her lips quirked in a slight smile. She'd never seen Alex grovel, and it was oddly endearing.

"But I hope you don't," he added. "Hate me, that is."

"I could never hate you," Lauren whispered, knowing it was true.

"I love you, Lauren." Alex moved forward and took her hands in his. "I want you to be my wife. My life won't be complete without you by my side."

"What about the baby?"

"The baby will be an extra bonus." His smile softened. "In fact, I've fantasized about what it would be like to have you as my wife and a child of our own."

Her heart started to sing. "You really love me?"

"I do." The look in his eyes brushed away the last of her doubts. "And if you give me the chance, I'll prove it to you. Every day. Every hour. Every minute of the rest of your life."

This time when she met his gaze, Lauren let the love that was in her heart show. "You know if we do marry, my mother will forever think I followed her advice and trapped myself a prince."

"Let her have her fantasy." Alex gently brushed back a strand of hair. "We'll live ours."

In that moment, happiness suddenly seemed within reach. "Oh, Alex, is this a dream?"

He pulled her into his arms and smiled. "If it is, I don't ever want to wake up."

"I love you, Alex."

"Then marry me," Alex said. "Say you'll share my life and I promise we'll live happily ever after."

"I always was a sucker for fairy-tale endings," Lauren murmured, her eyes wet with unshed tears.

As his lips lowered to hers and the baby moved inside her, Lauren realized that the fairy tale had only just begun.

Epilogue

One year later
Carpegnia Royal Palace

Sunlight streamed through the large leaded-glass windows just off the kitchen where Lauren, her mother and nine-month-old Prince Andrew were enjoying afternoon tea. Though Lauren had anticipated having a difficult time adjusting to life in a foreign country, Carpegnia had quickly become her home. Still, she loved it when friends and family came to visit.

"I'm so proud of you, honey," Clarice said.

Lauren took a sip of tea and smiled. She'd thought

her mother's eyes had glazed over when she was telling her about her latest foray into the Carpegnia educational system, but obviously her mother had been paying attention. "Working on that project for the Ministry of Education was a pleasure. It allowed me—"

"I wasn't talking about that," her mother interrupted. "Though I didn't understand half of what you told me, I'm sure you did an excellent job."

Andrew banged his hand on the high chair tray as if agreeing with his grandmother, a broad smile on his face.

"What then?" Lauren asked.

"All this." Her mother waved a hand. "I was just telling your father last night, we never gave you enough credit. You knew what you were doing all along. And you couldn't have done better for yourself. You've got a castle to call home, a fleet of luxury vehicles at your disposal and closets filled with the latest fashions. Plus you're married to a king." Clarice heaved a contented sigh. "You've got it all."

Over her mother's shoulders, Lauren saw Alex in the doorway and knew he'd overheard her mother's comments. They exchanged a smile of understanding.

Lauren shifted her gaze to her son jabbering happily in his high chair, his chubby hand waving the shortbread cookie like a scepter, before returning to her husband's face—familiar, known, increasingly beloved.

"You're right, Mother," Lauren said with a smile. "I really do have it all."

* * * * *

SILHOUETTE *Romance*®

presents a brand-new title in

CAROL GRACE's

heartwarming miniseries

Fairy Tale Brides

Cinderellie!

**(Silhouette Romance #1775)
Available July 2005
at your favorite retail outlet.**

Handsome venture capitalist Jack Martin had the
power to make Ellie Branson's dreams come true.
But could a man who wasn't looking for lasting
love really be her Prince Charming?

Also look for the next Fairy Tale Brides romance:

His Sleeping Beauty

(Silhouette Romance #1792, November 2005)

SILHOUETTE Romance®

Don't miss a moment of the

Blossom County Fair

Where love blooms true!

Rancher Cindy Tucker's challenge? Transforming from tomboy to knockout. Her prize? The cowboy who has haunted her dreams for years. Will he see her in a different light? Find out in:

A Bride for a Blue-Ribbon Cowboy
by JUDY DUARTE

Silhouette Romance #1776
Available July 2005

And the fun continues at the Blossom County Fair!

Flirting with Fireworks (SR #1780)
by TERESA CARPENTER
Available August 2005

The Sheriff Wins a Wife (SR #1784)
by JILL LIMBER
Available September 2005

Her Gypsy Prince (SR #1789)
by CRYSTAL GREEN
Available October 2005

If you enjoyed what you just read,
then we've got an offer you can't resist!

Take 2 bestselling
love stories FREE!

Plus get a FREE surprise gift!

Clip this page and mail it to Silhouette Reader Service™

IN U.S.A.	IN CANADA
3010 Walden Ave.	P.O. Box 609
P.O. Box 1867	Fort Erie, Ontario
Buffalo, N.Y. 14240-1867	L2A 5X3

YES! Please send me 2 free Silhouette Romance® novels and my free surprise gift. After receiving them, if I don't wish to receive anymore, I can return the shipping statement marked cancel. If I don't cancel, I will receive 4 brand-new novels every month, before they're available in stores! In the U.S.A., bill me at the bargain price of $3.57 plus 25¢ shipping and handling per book and applicable sales tax, if any*. In Canada, bill me at the bargain price of $4.05 plus 25¢ shipping and handling per book and applicable taxes**. That's the complete price and a savings of at least 10% off the cover prices—what a great deal! I understand that accepting the 2 free books and gift places me under no obligation ever to buy any books. I can always return a shipment and cancel at any time. Even if I never buy another book from Silhouette, the 2 free books and gift are mine to keep forever.

210 SDN DZ7L
310 SDN DZ7M

Name	(PLEASE PRINT)	
Address		Apt.#
City	State/Prov.	Zip/Postal Code

Not valid to current Silhouette Romance® subscribers.

Want to try two free books from another series?
Call 1-800-873-8635 or visit www.morefreebooks.com.

* Terms and prices subject to change without notice. Sales tax applicable in N.Y.
** Canadian residents will be charged applicable provincial taxes and GST.
All orders subject to approval. Offer limited to one per household.
® are registered trademarks owned and used by the trademark owner or its licensee.

SROM04R

©2004 Harlequin Enterprises Limited

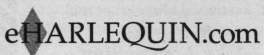

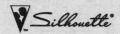

SPECIAL EDITION™

presents a new six-book continuity

MOST LIKELY TO...

**Eleven students. One reunion.
And a secret that will change everyone's lives.**

On sale July 2005

THE HOMECOMING HERO RETURNS

(SE #1694)

by bestselling author

Joan Elliott Pickart

Former college jock David Westport was convinced he had it all—a beautiful wife, two wonderful kids and a good business in his North End neighborhood. Sandra Westport loved her husband dearly but was positive that he did have one regret—letting her sudden pregnancy derail his chances at a pro baseball career ten years ago. And when a college professor revealed a secret that threw all the good in David's life into shadow, Sandra feared her marriage was over. Could David rebuild his shattered dreams without losing the love of his life?

Don't miss this emotional story—only from Silhouette Books.

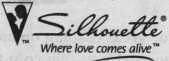

Where love comes alive™

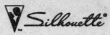
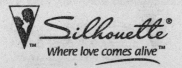

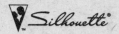

SPECIAL EDITION™

is proud to present a dynamic new voice in romance, Jessica Bird, with the first of her Moorehouse family trilogy.

BEAUTY AND THE BLACK SHEEP

Available July 2005

The force of those eyes hit Frankie Moorehouse like a gust of wind. But she quickly reminded herself that she had dinner to get ready, a staff (such as it was) to motivate, a busines to run. She didn't have the luxury of staring into a stranger's face.

Although, jeez, what a face it was.

And wasn't it just her luck that *he* was the chef her restaurant desperately needed, and he was staying the summer....

Where love comes alive™

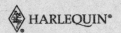